ETHOSBOT

S Sky, MS

This is a work of fiction. Incidents, entities, characters, and dialogue were conjured by the author's imagination. Resemblance to organizations or people is unintentional and coincidental.

ISBN 979-8-9886991-3-2

To my highly intuitive daughter who encouraged me to keep writing from the get-go with the very first chapter of the trilogy, *Sage and the Crystal Bot.* Her seemingly insignificant affirmation set the journey for fiction writing. I am truly thankful that, in her youth, my daughter dragged me into the equestrian world of which I knew nothing.

Contents

Chapter 1

SANDSTORM

In daylight, *TuramaliScape* glowed in the distance. The radiance was a surreal mix of earthy greens and flowing cobalt blue waters with a backdrop of sand dunes and red rock buttes. Although curvilinear, ultra-modern concrete structures on the campus were prominent, they eerily augmented the glow. Perhaps the emanation came from what lay inside.

TuramaliScape was born of the brazen effects of the turamali eco-bot that subtly gave way to righteous attention to ecology and community. Acquired thought transference or telepathy from the effects of the eco-bot pulled people together in mysterious ways. In truth, all life was intent on interrelating and crafting ways to thrive.

Fitting the mandate of reinvigoration, *Turamali Innovative Arts (TIA)* led the massive undertaking with a few other nations joining the *TuramaliScape* project. Exploration into innovative biologics and crystal healing was trendy with some feeling compelled to engage. Everyone wanted in on the concept of a business and residential development with turamali as the centerpiece.

Despite the cityscape being active for over a decade, the view remained captivating. It was an architectural wonder born of turamali, or generically the tourmaline crystal. Combined with the synthetically engineered botanical virus, it spawned revitalization of a dying planet.

The cityscape appeared unfazed betraying nothing of the EthosBot, nor the engineers' clandestine effort in the high Southwestern desert. The meddling in intelligent life may have gone too far spurring some to action.

Here, the wind perpetually reshaped the burnt sienna sand dunes. It was the perfect environment for the energy harmonizer. The contraption was quite novel, designed to capture solar and electromagnetic energies through a combination of photovoltaic cells and a modified magnetic induction process. They confirmed operability, and then carefully concealed the device — which was tricky, not due to its size, but reflectance.

The early autumn sun had the engineering team sweating through their T-shirts. Undeterred by desert-worthy shoes, the microfine sand particles found their way inside, niggling against toes further adding discomfort to hot feet. Feverish heat and irritation aside, phase one of their covert mission was accomplished.

One of the particularly vocal members shouted in vehemence as he faced *TuramaliScape.* "We feel you Ethos. And we're comin' for ya!" The others silently joined in by raising their water bottles in salute. For them, it was too hot to shout. Time to head back to civilization.

♦

"Biomagnetic medicine. An entire field dedicated to diagnosing and treating illness, and all based on normal electrophysiology. The Radiance and Assault Crystal BioBots have been godsends healing common ailments and tackling infectious diseases. ... Hard to imagine scads of doctors and healthcare professionals in so many disciplines only twenty years ago. All they did was fight disease and pain relentlessly. Everyone had something or another to treat. What a disaster that must have been ..."

As the trail widened, Cali pulled alongside her twin brother, Kalen, jabbering animatedly. Her caramel brown braid rested between her shoulder blades. Outdoor escapades had tanned her smooth olive complexion. Seeking a late afternoon adventure, the teens now meandered on their trusty steeds several miles from the hacienda.

"EthosBot, though ..." Cali pondered. "It's dicey messing with cognition and emotion when we really don't know for certain how the original botanical virus and tourmaline crystal created widespread telepathy. I mean, we know about psychoactive receptors, but create a specific bot to tinker purposefully with neurotransmitters and neurons? Kalen, it's a Pandora's box of lurking unknown evil. We need to stop it."

"Cali, you're so dramatic and impulsive! Just like mom ..." Kalen loved his sister, but she was impetuous. Although Cali meant to be courageous, Kalen believed she was too often simply looking for trouble.

Raking his dark brown wavy hair with his fingers, he sighed. "I agree with you, though. Our normal biomagnetic energy field is one thing. It's another to add a nanobot with its own geochemical properties hoping to alleviate anxiety and depression. The Radiance BioBot bestows glowing health. The Assault series attacks microorganisms that make us ill. But a brain bot? ... The world has gone along thus far because mental health has been the last frontier for Crystal BioBot therapy. I guess most of us are at least half crazy enough to need such a bot."

Kalen laughed at his last comment prompting a smirk from Cali. Kalen was christened as Sami but quickly adopted his middle name, Kalen. It was a name of Gaelic origin which meant 'keeper of the keys', pure and slender — all which Sami Kalen embodied. His mother teased he held the key to unlock hearts, while his father believed he held the keys to so much more.

"*Turamali Innovative Arts.* The Ethos clinical trials are endless, spanning years. The other bots were developed in mere months." Kalen continued contemplating aloud. "Too, Mom grows increasingly quiet about the work she's doing there with the team. Feels weird. Why are the results so nebulous? All that's reported is just that people change in the clinical trials. Change … change how? The reporting of clinical outcomes by physicians is couched in medical word-weaving with provisos that mean … what exactly? … Someone needs to put an end to Ethos. Why not us? We've certainly concocted a scheme that should work."

Sometimes, Kalen wondered if he was still trying to convince himself of the idea to stop the bot, or if he simply lacked the moxie that Cali possessed. The conversation ended, but the plotting and intention did not.

The seventeen-year-old twins were the offspring of Sage Amaris Casander, the long-ago purported eco-savior of life on Earth. Purported, as in the minds of youth, nearly two decades ago seemed like eons. Rightfully, their mother, Sage, was merely one bot-teamer on the Biologics & Intelligent Life Team who created the crystal-driven eco-bot which resulted in astounding rejuvenation of Earth — albeit with alarming, unintended effects on brain neurotransmitters. Was their mother truly the eco-savior of yore? It was difficult to believe sometimes.

However, Cali and Kalen both believed their mother deserved due credit. Cali recollected the bedtime stories about how it all began. She knew the history well.

Sage had been pushed to the brink of an ethical dilemma and she chose. *Coyote* had crossed her path far too often with the haunted stare and thin bedraggled body. Alone in her valiant bold action, Sage secretively launched the virus-laden bots to save botanical life. Thus, she saved Earth and so much more.

From environmental devastation, the synthetically engineered DNA virus revitalized lifeforms, first giving rise to greenery. Restoration of flora and crops meant people and animals had much needed robust food sources. Along with restored health came the uncanny, unintended phenomenon of thought transference, simply referred to as telepathy. Thus, the drop of the eco-bot onto a bleak planet Earth altered life forever — astoundingly and yet strangely.

Although the biotech company had 'turamali' wrapped in every copyright and trademark possible, it fell victim to category creation or genericization. Linguistically, turamali evolved from its crystal and bot brand to true cultural integration as the term denoted anything related to crystal phenomena, such as Turamali Telepathy, Turamali Life, Turamali Festival, and more. Thus, literary experts nitpicked turamali versus Turamali, but no one cared.

Soon though, people became somewhat confused by the biotechnology — either never fully understanding the original virus rejuvenation mechanism, or just simply neglecting the primary virus-driven process and instead focusing on the new-fangled crystal biotechnology to heal all.

Cali and Kalen leaned forward on their horses wanting to meander further into the lush desert. Cali rode Sabino, a gentle, highly attuned buckskin mare. Kalen rode Kona, a thoroughbred quarter horse cross.

Formerly her mother's horse, Sabino was now pushing twenty years. Engineered at the time Sage had conceived the twins, the Radiance BioBot uniquely healed bone and joint. For Sabino, it meant having the strength and stamina of half her calendar age. The sweet mare had also blossomed with not just simple thought transference, but indeed a discerning ability to wield psychic skills.

As the twins grew, so did Cali's connection with Sabino. It wasn't as if Cali usurped her mother's relationship with her equine companion, but by seven or eight years of age, it was clear to Sage that Sabino was meant to carry Cali. Bayani Casander, their father, had sensed it too. There was no sadness or loss. What Sage and Sabino had would never be diminished or fail. It was simply the universe guiding Cali and Sabino into a physical and soul connection meant to be. In awe, Bayani and Sage watched the soul-building of their head-strong daughter with an angelic four-legged.

Upper body and leg strength finessed over years of riding, Cali rode without a bridle. Instead, she had a leather halter on Sabino with the lead rope loosely circled around the mare's neck. Nestled in the mane, the lead rope rocked gently as they rode. Cali preferred an English saddle and now used a trendy lightweight model. She could have gone bareback, but longer rides were just more comfortable with saddle and stirrups. With ingrained seat and leg cues, Cali comfortably steered Sabino as telepathy added guidance and conversation.

EthosBot is here. Sabino, her horse, interjected with clarity. *In the wind, it pulsates through the ground.*

Cali was immediately intrigued by Sabino's bizarre, cautionary note. *TIA* is nearby with Ethos certainly being developed and tested there. However, Cali thought, what do the wind and ground have to do with the EthosBot? Strange. Sabino is clairsentient, but normally her *sensing* and thought transference are plausible.

Easy, Kona. You'll catch the log jumps on our return.

Holding the reins of a bitless bridle loosely in his hands, Kalen thought transferred to Kona. The bay gelding held the spirit of a sport horse — one that loves a gallop on soft sandy earthen pathways and airborne flight across any object or jump.

Not about the log jumps. Sabino feels it too. Ethos is here. Energy field coming. With this foretelling thought transference, Kona danced sideways.

In response, Kalen tensed. His well-muscled, toned stature matched Kona's athleticism, but Kona's current behavior was a déjà vu moment. Early on, Kalen had survived frightful moments of Kona's agility and eager spirit. He tumbled out of the saddle twice and then never again. Under Bayani, his astutely equine-adept father, Kalen had been *selected* for Kona and vice versa. The young rider's contradictory sensations of being magnetically drawn to Kona and equally surviving the horse's high energy and power soon dissipated. As telepathic communication between rider and horse refined, Kalen and Kona became as inseparable as Cali and Sabino.

"Cali, Sabino forewarning you? Kona says Ethos is here. Something's coming. You feel it?"

Tilting her head, Cali murmured just loud enough for her brother to hear. "Our horses *know.* The air, the wind stirring. A storm? The ground beneath us vibrates every so subtly."

Having made it to their destination, they came to a halt, side by side, at the edge of the mesa overlooking *TuramaliScape.* Despite their horses' palpable tension, the cityscape appeared placid hinting at nothing awry nor of Ethos.

T-Scape was strategically built across acres of vast rolling sienna sand dunes, intertwined with wide open spaces for gatherings and recreation. Light gray concrete buildings boasted distinctive curvilinear elements with rooftops and façades sporting waveforms that construed flowing — as in the flow of Turamali Telepathy. Apertures of various shapes and in various locations in each structure were purposefully asynchronous, constructed with engineering acumen for optimal natural light based on the building's cardinal direction. Whether designed for business or residence, the concept of space was quite amazing. Developers left nothing to tradition.

Interiors retained concrete ceilings, floors, and walls. Bold soothing water features were interspersed with living plant walls. To warm the senses from the gray stone architecture, the poured concrete floors were infused with earthen colors. Furniture and décor revived the spirit. Despite these design elements, some believed building interiors were too tranquil, not instigating vigor and innovation but instead a state of Turamali Bliss.

On the edge of campus, a manmade canal system for irrigation and drinking water stretched across the desert as far as the eye roamed. It, too, was an extraordinary architectural feat designed equally for beauty and function. Crystals clarified water streaming from higher elevations and were neatly positioned at the sides and bottom of the canal. The ice blue water was — no pun intended — crystal clear. It conjured thirst just to behold it.

A concrete promenade weaved canal-side with long stretches of intermittent, arced structures designed for shade and aesthetics. Indeed, more turamali-inspired wave and flow.

Beyond the sienna beach sand enveloping the community, the land transitioned to iron oxide-rich mesas and buttes. Dreamscape *TuramaliScape,* but nonetheless real. Telepathy kept everyone grounded and communicating. At least for now.

It was here on the trail amidst canopies of mesquite, palo verde, pinyon pine, and juniper that Kalen and Cali frequently carried on telepathic conversations with wildlife. Now, a few miles distant from the hacienda, they heard familiar dialogue. The voices of *Coyote* and *Cougar,* touchstones of the family for interspecies communiques, were particularly free-flowing and perceptible out in the open away from other distractions. Now, as Cali and Kalen studied the *T-Scape* horizon, *Coyote* and *Cougar* mimicked their horses' warning.

Ground pulsates. Air stirs. Storm ... dust devils. Coming ... coming now ... We run. The message from *Coyote* to Cali and Kalen was distinctly clear and urgent.

Both horses' ears were intently forward in listening mode. Kona sidestepped and pawed with one front hoof alerting his trail companions. Then both horses' ears twitched repeatedly — one ear forward, the other back — sorting out the source of barely perceptible sound and wind agitation.

Cali turned to Kalen with a whisper and hesitation, "Kalen, it feels ... catastrophic ... from *T-Scape.*" If something catastrophic was transpiring, should they dismount and hide? Gallop away?

Eerily, brisk wind suddenly whipped hair and mane. Until this point, the late afternoon ride had been warm for early autumn with the air unusually serene. The sudden shift in wind paralleled the discomfort of their steeds and the odd messaging from *Coyote* and *Cougar*. Adding to the odd and portentous moment, the scent of burning pinyon and mesquite trees filled their senses. A wildfire?

Senses conflicted. They saw the steadfast strength of a concrete cityscape combined with an uncanny wind and foreboding telepathic messages. Danger was imminent. What to believe when all felt mysteriously suspended in time and space? Yet, the moment ached for action.

In unison, the twins sat taller in their saddles taking short tentative breaths with muscles flexing. Still looking toward the distant cityscape, the fine hairs of their arms tingled followed by an intense prickling of their entire scalp. Further provoked by the unseen, their hands twitched and chests tightened. Distinct from the breeze, their horse's forelock and mane separated into fine hairs, elevating and lightly dancing in the air.

Brisk breeze transitioned to repeated gusts mixed with desert sand. The air bristled with strange but fierce energy, while fine sand particles pelted skin and coat. Although experienced in haboobs or sandstorms, this onslaught was different. Kona and Sabino knew it. The horses tensed for motion, simultaneously telepathing, *Retreat. Gallop. Now.*

"Stampede. Cal, stampede!"

Instinctively and without rider direction, Sabino and Kona turned abruptly putting the sandstorm and pelting grains at their hindquarters. In the sudden retreat, Cali and Kalen were nearly unseated.

At the same moment, the previous distant rumble intensified becoming a thunderous windstorm charged with unnerving and disorienting electromagnetic energy. The ground rolled and vibrated.

Cali shouted into the tumult of wind and pounding of animals racing by. "What's happening?"

"Ride with the wind ... and the animals!" Kalen pulled

ahead at a faster gallop, knowing that his gelding would be taking the jumps with ferocity. Sabino would jump the logs and rails, but with Cali in the saddle, the mare would hold a measured pace and takeoff even in the face of danger — a bit different from Kalen's all-out racing style. Kona's strength and endurance led the return to the hacienda.

Wildlife who roamed the high desert stampeded en masse away from *TuramaliScape*. Coyote packs raced, weaving between trees and ground cover. Cougar prides dashed deftly across outcrops and the nearby mesa. Contributing to the ground thunder were wild horse herds and safari animals. As interspecies telepathic alliances ascended within a few short years after the errant eco-bot launch, exotics were set free into the wild thriving in harmony with existing ecosystems.

As the tempest surged, human and horse were pelted mercilessly by fine sand particles that stung eyes and bare skin or coat. Despite sunshades and clothing pulled over noses, vision became unbearable and breathing stifled.

Cali and Kalen heard everything and yet nothing. Branches bent and groaned. Thundering hoofbeats and stomping intertwined with terrifying howling, trumpeting, and neighing. The cacophony of sound competed with particles of sand pelting their outer ears, becoming equally discernable and muddled. *How can this be?*

Strangely, the air sizzled as if transmitting electrical voltage. Muscles and joints ached and burned, as if the very inhaled scent of pinyon and mesquite wildfire seared to their core. The twins wanted to cower from the pain assaulting their senses. In seconds, the onslaught of noise and swirling wind overwhelmed normal equilibrium. Dizziness and disorientation overcame them.

With each stride, their leg and hip muscles turned flaccid, relaying to Sabino and Kona that all was not well with their riders. The teens struggled to remain upright on their steeds and maintain mental focus. Finding balance or safety in the moment seemed impossible. Being inundated as well by the cacophonous and disabling onslaught, Kona and Sabino deftly navigated the tumult shifting from gallop to restrained canter to tentative walk.

Sabino, help me! With hearing and mental faculties fading, Cali felt herself slipping into oblivion. Her vision blurred and she fought to stay upright in her saddle. *Sabino, Kalen …* In a last conscious effort, Cali reached forward in an embrace of Sabino's neck with one hand still clutching a fistful of mane.

Tighten your legs. Stay with me, Cali …

Under the same spell, Kalen and Kona slowed to a halt ahead of Cali and Sabino. As quickly as the storm and ensuing tumult had arisen, it dissipated, leaving the four companions confused and worn as adrenaline drained. The sandstorm had artistically peppered life with fine iron oxide-rich and gypsum sand particles — head-to-toe, muzzle to hindquarter, leaf to bark, flower to cactus pad. Desert life emerged spray painted with a misty coat of sand.

Kalen used the sleeve of his shirt to rub away irritating sand from his eyes and mouth. His light beard felt scratchy. Kona's bay color was now mottled with a coppery sheen from the zillion specks of soil blasted by the haboob. Kalen shook his head and rubbed Kona's neck in appreciation for the steady ride during the odd and raucous storm. He turned Kona to face Cali. Seeing his sister weak, pale, and trying to push off Sabino's neck, he pulled up alongside.

"Cali! Can you hear me? Cal?" *You fainted.*

"Dizzy. Wobbly. Need … need to lie …" As she spoke in single words, Kalen quickly dismounted rushing to guide his sister gently to the ground. She fell limply to her knees, moving her hands forward in the soft sand trail as if to grab hold of something solid. Kalen knelt on one knee adjacent to Cali placing a hand consolingly on her shoulder.

Shouts suddenly were heard on the trail ahead. Leaning forward, he massaged his temple and ran his free hand through his thick wavy hair. *What now? Cali, stay still. Sabino ...* Kalen's thought transference ended. No need to say more to Sabino, as the mare bent her legs, neatly folding them beneath her as she lay protectively within just a few feet of Cali.

"Help! Kalen, Cali! I *sense* you're here ... Zane is hurt." The yelling trailed off.

Rather than shouting in return, he shook off the disorientation and telepathed. *Zia, you're near the trail? I'm coming.*

No reply from Zia. Strange, Kalen thought.

Grabbing the reins of the bitless bridle in one hand and placing the other hand flat against the knee roll of the saddle, Kalen slouched resting his forehead on Kona's sweaty neck. Taking in the comforting scent of his horse, he needed a moment to regain stability and focus. I'm so drained from that electrifying burst. My chest feels tight. Heart feels fluttery, arrhythmic.

Dad, mom, what happened to us? Kalen attempted contact.

With a deep intake of breath, he gathered wits and strength remounting Kona with effort. He thought, I better ride to Zia and Zane. Don't know how far ahead or what trouble they're in.

As he pushed to find his best friends, Kalen resumed telepathy, attempting to discover if his parents were okay and what weird emanation came from *T-Scape*. No need to share any alarm about their situation yet with his parents. Kalen took pride in showing his father that he could handle anything thrown at him. *Mom, Dad? Can't hear either of you.*

Kalen, your mother's telepathy is stymied by TIA and an apparent force field surrounding the campus. On the ranch, we're dealing with animal injuries from the stampede. Get home with your sister … and your unexpected compadres. Need you.

Sensing his rider was shaken, unsteady, and distractedly sorting thought messages, Kona picked up a bright forward walk rather than a trot. Kalen's typical strong, definitive leg and seat were surprisingly weak. Intermingled with debilitating electrical emanations, the haboob had achieved more than disorientation.

Easy, Kalen. Defiance and Desperado are just ahead, Kona telepathed.

Defiance, a quarter horse, was Zia's trusty mount, and Desperado, an American Paint, was Zane's. Kalen rode about a half mile on the trail toward home when he spotted Zia anxiously pacing and waving her arm. Adjacent to a mesquite in a ground tie, her horse Defiance stood, ears alert with the reins resting forward on the ground. Forced to fidget from the sand pelting, Defiance bent forward rubbing his eye firmly against his foreleg, and then snuttered trying to dislodge irritating dirt and runny nostril excretions.

As Kona halted, Zia strode toward Kalen placing her hand on the calf of his leg still in the stirrup. She needed to feel his strength. Their eyes met with immediate *speak*.

"I'm here, Zia."

"I'm scared, Kalen. Zane … he's fallen … hit his head against the trunk of a palo verde. Desperado didn't take too well to whatever just happened out here. The mare bolted."

Zia's face was taut with desert dirt smeared on her face and hands. Her eyes were wide betraying deep fear for her brother.

No sooner had Zia finished speaking when Kalen caught Desperado's movement among the canopy of trees and desert brush. Quickly dismounting, he rushed after Zia. Several yards off the trail and still dazed, Zane was struggling to sit upright. Zia fell into place behind her brother, supporting his back and kneeling firmly against him while cradling his shoulders.

Zane was seventeen like Kalen and Cali. His pursuit of martial arts had given him a toned muscled physique, and over time it curtailed his namesake zany character. At least, the discipline had honed his easy going, quick-to-laugh nature channeling it to fewer stunts and jokes.

His sister, Zia was nearly sixteen. Her medium brown bob was now a sandy mess of tangles. She appeared slight next to her brother, especially as she pressed up against his back using all her strength to support him.

Kalen mentally ran through what his father had taught him about assessing falls from a horse. He wanted to remain calm and upbeat, but still properly take the right steps to safely get his friend home or get help to come to them.

"Dude, bro. What the heck happened?" Kalen knelt in front of Zane. "Do you need to lie down? If you're going to sit up, you're talking to me. Got that?"

Zane tried to twist sideways as if to loosen his neck and shoulders. He grabbed for Zia's arm to steady himself.

"Dizzy, headache, but ... want to sit up ... easier to ... breathe."

"No laughing now at my questions. Tell me your name and what day it is."

Sighing and smirking, Zane replied to Kalen in stuttered

words.

"Look at me, buddy. Show me those girl-chasing eyes." Kalen chuckled.

He observed the struggle from his best friend and swore to himself to keep the exchange as light-hearted as possible. The situation was serious, but avoiding fear was equally important to keep panic at bay. Zia was trembling as she supported her brother, and it was debatable if Zane would pass the test to ride out of there unassisted.

Kalen gently grabbed Zane's shoulders and studied his gaze. Kalen briefly caught his friend's visual attention, but then Zane's focus and head drifted sideways. He couldn't assess the pupils in that timespan or in the current light and shadow. His friend had trouble focusing and was dazed by the injury — that much appeared evident.

Still grasping his friend's shoulders firmly, Kalen pursued in a hopeful note, "Breathing better now?" He noticed how Zane slouched to one side but systematically attempted to straighten until pain pulled him into a slouch.

"Breathing okay but not … pain … ribs. Maybe … can stand."

"Wait a bit longer. I have a few more questions. Are you bleeding anywhere?"

Without waiting for a response and turning to Zia, Kalen tilted his head, "Any cuts, lacerations?"

"A small patch of dried blood on the back of his head, but nothing else that I can see."

"Zany … hey … you chilly, cold?"

"Now that you mention it … feeling like a sss…oak in our seg…rid … hot spring would be nice … Ready to stand. Get me rr…ome … Where's Desper…d … that crazy P...int?"

Verbal conversation challenged and noted.

A couple of tears streaked down Zia's cheeks making

funny zigzag lines following the sand dust particles on her face.

Kalen winked encouragingly at Zia, "You got this girl. Let's get him up. We need to figure out if he can ride Desperado, or if you lead his horse, while I take him on Kona. I'm not sure I want to wait for help to come to us. I've got to go back and get Cali and Sabino. They're just down the trail. The field reverberations messed with Cali enough to cause her to faint. Hopefully, her head has cleared, and she's able to ride."

Zane was unsteady on his feet leaning heavily at first on Kalen. Haltingly, they moved stepwise toward the open trail while Zia commandeered the Paint. Desperado was not a difficult or spooky horse — at least not under typical circumstances. She had a good mind and disposition. Along with the stampede, the strange out-of-the-blue sandstorm, stampede, and electrical disruption clearly set the Paint off. Sometimes, stuff just happens on a horse, with a horse, despite equine training or rider expertise.

Kalen asked Zia to grab his jacket from the daypack hooked to Kona's saddle. Together they got the jacket and hood around Zane. Kalen knew he needed to get some warmth to Zane's upper body; especially since they were not keeping him flat or elevating his legs to prevent shock — which still concerned Kalen, but he said and telepathed nothing. They needed to move. Daylight was fading.

With all three friends and their steeds standing on the trail, they quickly debated the best course of action. Ideally, Zane should ride a horse, as riding double was hard on a horse's back — no matter what the Westerns of yore alleged. Kona could take both Kalen and Zane, but only if no other option seemed feasible.

Thus, Kalen and Zia needed to feel confident that Zane

could sit upright and steady alone in his saddle as he rode back to the hacienda at a brisk walk. Furthermore, should Zane stick with his horse or ride Kona or Zia's horse? Was the Paint steady enough now or still spooked — at all, in any way?

Although uncomfortable with rib and head pain, Zane's senses appeared to clear. He spoke now without stuttering or slurring, but with obvious hesitation as he seemed to sort out words. "Zia, you take the Paint home. I'll ride ... Def... iance. I know him. He's as steady as ... he ... didn't bolt."

"He's right, Kalen. Zane and I trade off riding each other's horse all the time. I'll take the Paint, Desperado, and settle her. Do you want me to go back and help with Cali?"

No sooner were the words out when Cali and Sabino sauntered up toward the motley group. What a sight Cali beheld. Although covered with a sandy haboob film and smudges across his jeans, Kalen stood tall with quiet control. Equally peppered in a sandy haze, Zia appeared disheveled but clear-headed. Tear streaks were apparent, but her visible trembling had stopped. Attention drawn to Cali, Zane struggled to mount Defiance alone, as the quarter horse turned his head nudging the unsteady human being.

"Looks like someone needs a little help, guys," Cali nodded up ahead. "Defiance can tuck his legs under and lay down for Zane to mount."

In relief at seeing his sister with her normal wit and wisdom, Kalen spun toward Zane to prevent any further mishap. Kalen gave Defiance a 'down' signal, and the horse willingly obliged. Kalen guided his friend into the saddle, praying for his steadiness and a safe journey back. With Defiance up and the wounded rider sinking into quiet submission to the horse's strength, Kalen telepathed to the quarter horse, *Take him to the hacienda. His father awaits with mine.*

Kalen firmly rubbed the horse's neck and gave Zane's leg a squeeze. "I'm right behind you, buddy. I'll be riding next to you the whole way." Sensing his friend's pain, Kalen added endearingly, "Kemosabe."

Zane gazed at Kalen, tightening his lips at the obvious pain, while nodding at the affable term the two shared.

As Zia mounted the Paint, Cali came up beside her. "Does señorita Desperado feel okay under you? Edgy still? A bit of dance left in our Paint?"

"High-spirited, spooked still. I can feel it." Zia eyed Cali revealing simultaneous tension and fatigue with the situation. She envied how easily Cali could stretch and flex her riding skills from steed to steed.

Once, Cal had taken on a young Arabian that no one else would ride. But Cali did. She made it look as if the two were strategically paired as they trotted, cantered, and even took low jumps. Upon demand, Cali spun magic on the worst-tempered or crazy-energized four-legged. Zia admired Cali and loved her dearly, but ... *Why can't some Cali magic rub off on me?*

To break the pervasive nervousness and equally encourage Zia, Cali laughed, "So, girlfriend, Sabino will set a steady pace for us. Not to worry." *Magic, Zia, you have it. You just don't recognize it.*

Hearing the telepathed thought, Zia smoothed wayward strands of hair behind her ear and laughed too. *Zia magic. Huh. I'll take it.*

The sun was setting fast behind rolling hills, shadows lengthened, and the trail darkened. The girls took the lead toward home, eventually shifting to a canter. The group decided the sooner some of the party could move closer to help, the better. Kalen rode adjacent to Zane keeping a careful eye on his friend.

Both brother-sister pairs had contacted their parents by telepathy in fitful segments. Hence, it was no surprise that about three miles from the hacienda, Bayani gallantly loped up to the teens. There were several other riders with him, all wearing reflective gear with small lights attached to the tack. Unless necessary, the well-seasoned caballeros avoided bright flashlights or headlamps as they disturbed the horse's vision. The rescue posse had some fortune on their side tonight, as the full moon cast enough light to distinguish well-worn trail from prickly brush.

In thoughtless spontaneity, Cali's eyes watered at the sight of her father. In unison, they pulled up together. Knowing what Cali had been through, Bayani smiled wide with extreme pride.

"At last, Dad, you're here," Cali whispered to herself. Her shoulders relaxed. "Dad, behind us. Zane needs help."

"Cali, Zia, keep moving. Carson! Guide these riders home!" Carson knew it would be him to escort the girls, leaving Bayani and the others to assist Zane and Kalen.

Even in the semi-darkness, Carson spied Cali's fatigue. He approached the girls inquiring, "You señoritas okay? Understand the sandstorm and stampede were nasty where you were." He wanted to ride adjacent to Cali and reach out for her hand, but he knew this wasn't the time or place. He had to give due attention to Zia as well.

With a glance at Zia, Carson felt something was off. "Zia, you okay on the Paint? We can switch horses. Not a problem."

With the greeting of the riders-to-the-rescue, Cali and Zia had slowed to a walk on their steeds. The sudden loud hooting of an owl caused the Paint to dance sideways, and Zia's upper body jostled unnerving her.

Aggravated by the Paint's lingering jumpiness, she asserted, "No, it's fine. I'm too tired to think about switching horses. Just get us home."

Carson nodded, but rode adjacent to Zia knowing his steed, Bandit, would calm the Paint, and with any luck, bring the rider solace too. Cali and Sabino followed the glimmer of Carson's reflective vest, and the path lit by the full moon as it rose high into the sky.

Almost home.

Chapter 2

HACIENDA

The hacienda was a sprawling ranch with open fields, arenas, barns, and of course, the main historic casa and a few smaller casitas. As barn manager, Bayani Casander had originally taken up residence in one of the adobe casitas with skip-peeled vigas, ample interior living space, and a front porch fit for morning java time and late-night stargazing.

Sometime during the twins' toddler years, the hacienda owners decided to take advantage of their age and affluence to travel to exotic locales. They asked Bayani and Sage to move their family into the main casa and run the entire estate. The associate hacienda manager, Carson, and a few of the barn hands with their small families kept residence in the casitas. This was not only welcomed but direly needed, as Turamali Life too often meant an unpredictable existence. In simple terms, an extended family of diverse backgrounds and skills resided on this unique pristine land.

Tonight, it was fortuitous that all this help was nearby and ready to meet the bedraggled and injured. Despite handling their own repercussions from the freak storm, an impromptu posse had been quickly assembled to rescue the teens.

As Cali and Kalen sauntered over a rise in the land, they spied flames from firepits located throughout the rambling property. String lights lit the casa and casitas. The glow of home and hearth permeated their souls. The scent of wood fire wafted on now innocent breezes.

Cali and Kalen's mom, Sage, and Zia's mother were the first to greet the girls and Carson. Carson caught Sage's gaze and gave a respectful nod to Cali's mother. Whatever Sage felt about Carson and her daughter being together, she did not reveal.

My sweet daughter, you're safe, was all that Sage could muster to telepath. A mother relinquishes incrementally, especially as the teen years track to adulthood. Then again, does a mother ever let go?

The riders dismounted. Cali and Zia hugged their moms, feeling pure relief wash over them as only maternal touch can do.

Carson and another rancher led the three horses toward the barn for untacking, feeding, and well-deserved rest. Even in the new world of animal freedom, domesticated equines often chose to stay in the barn they had come to know. Human caretakers still provided grass hay and ready access to fresh water. Stalls were open, gates meaningless, and herd mates were nearby. Horses of the rescue posse and those in the thick of the late afternoon tempest took respite at the hacienda tonight.

It was nearly another twenty long minutes before Bayani, Kalen, Zane, and the remaining posse posted over the nearby hill. Cali and Zia waited anxiously with their mothers. It appeared that one horse was riderless being led by another rider and his steed.

Firelight flickered off reflective gear. It was now evident why one horse was riderless. His horse stepping ever so carefully but agilely, Bayani held Zane in front of himself. Bayani had taken off his saddle, and simply ridden on the bareback pad with Zane slouched and nodding in front of him. Defiance, who had originally carried a compromised Zane, now simply accommodated two saddles while being deftly led by one of the caballeros.

At the property entrance, a vehicle approached. Announcing the arrival of more parents, slim high-terrain tires crunched on small stones. The Float3 hovercraft swept passed pavers, switching from hover mode to tire cushion and onto desert biocrust. The passenger door flung open, and Zane's father jogged briskly toward the arrival of the last riders approaching the ranch. The hovercraft pilot, Cyprus Desai, outwardly calm, followed the rush at a determined pace. Two federal agents sought their teens who bravely endured a strange Earth event, likely BioBot-instigated.

Carson had been watching for the return of the other riders, when he spied Kalen cantering up and dismounting in haste. No sooner had Bayani also pulled up adjacent to those anxiously awaiting when Carson raced forward joining Kalen. Together, they gently slid Zane from Bayani's hold and onto the ground. Carson's strong upper body hoisted the dazed limp teen into a weak stand, while Kalen moved quickly to support his buddy on the opposite side.

Finally at their son's side, both parents grabbed for him. Zane's father took his son's face in his hands and peered closely. Conscious but barely. *Zane, we're here.* To ease the emotional scare, he let his trained agent demeanor kick in and focused on his son's physical status.

Still astride his horse, Bayani exclaimed, "Get him to

Turamali Care. Likely got a nasty concussion."

"I'll transport you," Cyprus stepped out of the shadows. "I brought Zane's dad. We were working a case together when telepathic messaging began tumbling in." *Literally. From everywhere.*

Sage turned and hugged Cy. *Thank you, old friend.*

Cyprus Desai, the man-bun-wearing, federal agent extraordinaire had been instrumental in handling Sage's eco-terrorist saga. Over time, as others had, Cy and his romantic partner, Jen Clark, had slid into Sage's life becoming not simple acquaintances, but close companions and extended parents to Cali and Kalen. Jake Rivers and Kehlani Rose had also fatefully crossed Sage's path, also becoming extended parents earning the collective moniker 'fireside amigos'.

The fireside amigos — Sage, eco-savior and Bayani, equestrian; Jen, attorney and Cyprus, federal agent; Kehlani, spiritual Adept and Jake, park ranger — had all been drawn into the fantastical turamali rejuvenation phenomenon two decades ago, only to cross paths in serendipitous ways forging extraordinary deep friendships that would persist through tribulation and celebration, and the birth and rearing of Cali and Kalen.

As Carson and Kalen placed Zane in the back seat of the Float3, Zane's parents climbed in just as Cyprus fired up the craft. Kalen piloted Zia in her parents' vehicle, so that her family would have it after Cy left Zane and his parents at *T-Care.*

Z, Zaner's gonna be fine. Kalen gently brushed the sleeve of his shirt across Zia's cheek, trying to jostle fine tear-crusted desert dust from her complexion. Encouragingly, he clasped Zia's hand firmly. Her fitful trembling had abated, but her worn appearance from the late-day fiasco touched Kalen. He escorted Zia inside *Turamali Care*, then joined Uncle Cy.

Cyprus and Kalen returned to the hacienda in the FSPA (Federal Security and Pursuit Agency) Float3. Operating on piezoelectricity, the craft hummed along the turamali-infused roadway. Kalen's kinship with Cy was analogous to an uncle — or perhaps just as accurately as a second father. Finally in comfortable space, Kalen felt his eyes grow heavy.

"Rest, Kalen. You just saved your friend after some freakish storm." *I bet your mother has something to tell us about all this.* Unguarded, Cy had allowed the telepathic thought to spill out. Perhaps he should not have let it. Kalen needn't worry about his mother and bots tonight.

"My dad and you are so very strong, Uncle Cy. Between the two of you and Jake, I hope I learned well. I wish I could have done more for Zane. He became progressively weak on the ride back. I just ... he was so out of it ... You know, I need zany Zane, my goofball pal ..."

Succumbing to exhaustion, Kalen transitioned from verbal conversation to effortless telepathy. *First, the disorienting haboob, desert stampede, Cali struggling, and then everyone relying on me.*

Cyprus reached over jostling Kalen's shoulder. *You're a hero. You took care of the girls and your best buddy. I know you triaged him. Heard you. You forget I'm tuned in with you at an Adept level just as your father, Bayani.*

Gaining the skills of an Adept often took years. For most, thought transference was conferred by turamali-infused food and water with no further expansion of psychic skills. For a few, clairaudience, claircognizance, and clairsentience were bestowed by turamali. Some even gained clairvoyance, the ability to see future events. The onset of any psychic skill or combination of abilities was variable with no clear demographic correlations — other than being female which significantly increased the possibility of gaining skills beyond thought transference.

The physiologic basis, the variable impact on neurons and neurotransmitters, was unknown. To date, medical gurus simply did not know how or why some individuals swiftly gained expanded psychic skills while others did not. Furthermore, some had to work to refine whatever ability or abilities befell them, while others merely acquired them. An Adept was someone who wielded a combination of psychic skills and did so as an art.

When Cy and Kalen returned to the hacienda, they joined Sage and Bayani, catching the two parents as they spoke in subdued tones. The flames of the fire in the large camp-style pit were just beginning to dwindle. The barn crew must have fired up the logs when the posse left in search of the teens, knowing the tall flames would light their way home.

Kalen watched his mother as she appeared entranced by the low flames and glowing wood embers. She twirled her hair, as she often did when she felt lost. At least, that's what his mother had told Kalen one time when he asked about her quirky but characteristic habit. "Kalen, when I feel emotionally drained or lost in a sea of random thought, it's what I do. I fidget, Kalen — just like a little kid — like you!" Then she had tickled him until he found a way to scooch out, laughing and panting, from under her motherly grasp.

Bayani turned and took a few steps to greet his son. He had not had time before Kalen left with Zia, nor had he recovered fully from the tedious ride with Zane. Bayani gave Kalen one of his big bear hugs, embracing and rocking his son with pride. Kalen heard a familiar whisper from his father which prompted him to return the fierce hug.

After a few moments, feeling somewhat embarrassed in front of Uncle Cy by a too-long parental caress, Kalen gently pulled away.

"Dad, I'm sorry you had to carry Zane. It should have been me. I should have done it at the outset rather than allow him to ride back on Defiance."

Now, he eyed his father more carefully. He detected that his father had been fully spent by the effort of carrying a weakened, akimbo rider.

"You have unbelievable upper body and leg strength, even bareback on a horse, but you shouldn't have been tested tonight. Dad, thank you."

On occasion, Kalen was known to look out for his parents, almost in a caretaker role. Neither Sage nor Bayani needed their son to protect or worry about them, but they had raised a son who was not only self-reliant but socially conscious and mindful of others. Mostly, they were thankful this trait extended to his sister, Cali, who in their estimation needed an equal who could rein in her wacky notions and misplaced convictions.

Bayani pursed his lips, tilting his head, "That ol' quarter horse you and your sister tell me needs to be set free from work ... Yet tonight, Dakota performed like a rodeo champ. She's agile with an even-keeled spirit. The mare made carrying Zane possible."

Bayani felt more comfortable deflecting any reference to his endurance or age. It was easier to give his horse credit. Although the Radiance BioBot continued to award unparalleled vitality to the population, physical aging still crept forward for human and animal. Bayani was well into his fifth decade, and Sage too had recently passed the fifty-year mark.

"Speaking of my sister, where's Cali?" No sooner had he posed the question when Kalen realized — he did know. Raising his eyebrows and pushing out a sigh, he looked at the embers to avoid his parents' gaze.

Out of the corner of his eye, Kalen thought Uncle Cy was hiding a smirk. Cyprus, like the entire extended-parent group, knew full well about the couples — Cali & Carson, Kalen & Zia. With telepathy and *high knowing* or claircognizance, Uncle Cy & Aunt Jen, Uncle Jake & Aunt Kehlani knew of the twins' trysts. Innocent trysts, but nonetheless hot and bothered teenage love. The aunts and uncles along with parents had been quite tolerant. Zia and Zane were not faring as well with their parents.

After a few seconds of silence, his mom nudged, "Kalen, why don't you find Cali … and Carson … and let's all move inside. It's time I run through what happened today at *TuramaliScape*. Cy, you need to know, and Cali and Kalen should be informed too. There are some things I cannot hide from my sweet children …" His mother trailed off with a look of resignation and somberness.

Kalen, Carson should not be a part of the family and TIA work discussion. Wish him a kind good night. He was a great help to the posse, giving encouragement to Zia and aiding Zane. Kalen nodded at his mother and headed to Carson's casita on the property.

Although advised by her father not to go to, nor be seen at Carson's casita, Kalen knew his stubborn sister went anyway. At seventeen, Cali was in love with a twenty-five year-old, who was also the associate manager of the hacienda reporting directly to Bayani, her father. Not ideal in any respect.

Kalen knew the situation was strained, especially for their mother. After all, it was one rebel to another. Could the offspring of Sage Amaris, the brave eco-savior, be anything but another altruistic revolutionary? Or less dramatically and apropos in this instance, be anything but fiercely independent even regarding matters of the heart?

Our Cali ... how will this end? I feel it. Her impending tie to the EthosBot troubles me. Uneasiness tickles at the edge of my psyche. Kalen has found an easy rhythm in the teen years, but Cali is determined, obstinate, single-minded. This geostorm incident has made her more adamant about interfering with BioBot technology.

Not anticipating a response, Sage telepathed to Bayani and Cyprus. She had to share with those who'd been through the worst of the turamali debacle ... and indeed saved her ... what sometimes felt like eons ago but still haunted her. Surely, Cy, a federal agent, and Bayani, Cali's father, could prevent renegade action by their daughter. Sage added, *We can't control, but we can persuade.*

As Sage, Bayani, and Cy meandered toward the sprawling casa, Cy took Sage gently by the waist with one arm. Bayani was never offended by the endearing interactions of the fireside amigos. It was how they cared for one another and parented with an unusual rhythm and ease.

"Your rebel action almost two decades ago was deemed honorable. Granted, after a criminal investigation, telepathy and lifeforms gone wild, and your research team's unending task of surveillance and new bot creation ... your unsanctioned eco-bot launch was forgiven by those who held you accountable, and then celebrated worldwide for the true save of life that surely would have lost had you not stepped up.

"Sage, as the agent who pursued you and *Turamali Innovative Arts* mercilessly, I should be the worst critic. Your daughter ... Have you ever considered that Cali was meant to carry your legacy, but in her own way as turamali continues to weave life yet unimagined? She's going to need the rebellious, moralistic nature that you and Bayani bestowed on her. How else will your daughter save, fulfill her mission?"

Bayani was glad to see Cy trying to put Sage at ease with a perspective on history and their feisty daughter. What was Cy's last comment? Cali is meant to save? Save what? A mission? May the Higher Powers help us all.

Still holding Sage's waist, Cyprus reached across for Bayani with his free arm and pulled him into a shoulder caress. When the threesome reached the arched adobe portal with dangling chili pepper adornments, Cy begrudgingly released Sage and Bayani from the casual embrace. For a few moments as they strolled, Cyprus felt whole and calm — a respite from agent work and case files that would never close.

♦

Terracotta Saltillo tile covered the living space of the casa floor. It could easily have been the original flooring, but no one knew for certain. Worn smooth in many places by footsteps, it was cool and barefoot-easy. Decorative Talavera tiles of intricate design and color brought attention to archways and wall niches. Providing ceiling and vertical support, skip-peeled vigas polished the Southwestern ambiance.

Pueblo ladders held Navajo and Zapotec rugs, and Taos drums served as end tables holding modern lamps. An iron Spanish mission cross hung alongside watercolor and giclée numbered and signed prints of horses and open spaces of the Southwest. Overstuffed and cushioned equipale furniture was mixed with modern, cuddle-worthy family pieces. In the Age of Turamali and technology-driven modernism, this abode was a unique comfort and treasure.

Some of the furnishings were left by the hacienda owners, but Sage and Bayani added much of their own touch. They brought the green inside, so plants were placed around the rambling interior — from the living room and kitchen to dens and bedrooms, and finally to patios that were tandem with most of the bedrooms. If Southwest charm was a touchstone, the hacienda held it all — from warm earth tones to spiritual talismans and curios.

Magic and Marley, the resident dogs, greeted the family as they entered. The family dogs were chosen by the twins. As Cali and Kalen grew, they wanted their own playmates. Cali wanted to bring Sabino, her equine buddy, into her bedroom, but since that was not an option, a sweet canine pal fit the need. A trip to the local shelter was spontaneous one day, as Bayani and Sage were coerced by their pleading children.

Even in the Age of Turamali, animal shelters thrived, as not all animals had adapted to freedom in the wild. At the local shelter, Cali and Kalen each found their four-legged cuddle mate for home. Although Cali had been drawn to Magic and Kalen to Marley, the dogs became equally attached to both twins with the dogs randomly choosing their sleeping partner each night.

When Kalen returned with his sister to the casa, the cast of visitors had grown to include all the legendary fireside amigos — the extended parents or aunts and uncles. Joining the gathering in the hacienda living room and kitchen were Jen, Kehlani, and Jake. The scent of warm food and candles filtered throughout the space. Cali and Kalen were instantly reminded of their forgotten hunger and their need for solace.

As he prepared tacos with Bayani, Jake gave a shout of welcome to the twins. Kehlani and Jen immediately moved to embrace the teens.

In an immediate need to *read* the teens, Kehlani reached for one of Cali's hands with both of hers in a gentle but encompassing grasp. *You have much on your mind tonight. The odd storm plays in and out of conscious thought no matter how much you push it out. You fear for your friends. Mostly, you fear that your brother will follow your errant lead.*

Face drawn and in a semi-trance of disbelief, Cali stared at her aunt. The fine dust particles from the pelting storm gave Cali an owl-like appearance outlining the sunglasses now long gone. Aunt Kehl's uncanny perception felt unnerving tonight after all that had transpired. *Aunt Kehl, the EthosBot is out of control.*

Despite the teen's head-to-toe dusting in desert mayhem, Kehlani swiftly pulled Cali into an embrace. As if too fatigued or overwhelmed to return the hug, Cali limply placed her forehead against her aunt's shoulder.

In likewise sentiment and motion, Jen took Kalen gently at his elbows drawing him near. Seeing his identical dusty reddish-brown speckling and smudges, she softly laughed. Then she ran her hands from elbows to forearms taking in Kalen's energy and thoughts.

"Kalen, you carry the burdens of everyone here. It's not your job to worry about Uncle Jake and the animals. Not your job to worry about hiding your sister's intentions from Uncle Cyprus, and what the feds would do if they discovered your conversations. Too, your parents are the strongest people I know. Your fretting would do them no good." As if to punctuate her words, Jen squeezed Kalen's forearms.

Acknowledging his Aunt Jen's intuition and fervent advice, Kalen gently placed his hands on her shoulders following through with an innocent kiss to her cheek. "Love you, Aunt Jen. You're so insightful and terribly practical in every circumstance. I see why Cali admires you and Uncle Cy. But ..."

"But the shedding of burden-carrying is easier said than done, especially when that is what your nature draws you to do. Yet, I'll tell you this, Kalen dear. Your sister is going to need you before all of this is over, and if you're saddled with the cares of others, you'll lack the strength and focus to give your sister ... and your dear 'tryst and scheme' amigos ... what they need when the time demands it."

In awe of what he just heard Aunt Jen reveal, Kalen cocked his head sideways releasing his aunt's shoulders, and dropping his hands to his side. *How do you know ... know what's to come ... and 'tryst and scheme' such a curious term ...*

Playfully but with meaning, Jen placed her finger vertically across her lips in a cue of quiet and continued in a hushed tone. "I don't know the future. Neither do you nor any of us. But we can *sense* what is to come. As far as tryst and scheme — it's simply the words I *hear*. The rendezvous and plotting are your own. All your parent-mentors are aware, but we do not *know* intimate details. We don't invade."

In spooky twin fashion, Cali and Kalen concurrently stepped back from their respective aunt's emotional embrace to trade greeting their other aunt. Cali reached for Jen's hand, and Kalen reached into a hug with Kehlani also extending an endearing kiss to her cheek.

Over the years, Cali had enchantingly befriended Aunt Jen. Her aunt's legal mind always fascinated her — how she approached the world and finessed circumstances and the law to ethical conclusions. Aunt Jen, attorney at law, did not always win her cases per se … or did she? Even a loss on the books inevitably turned strangely to benefit those in need. Dubious justice and truth aside, her cases ended in a life or lives being freed; albeit the notion of freedom emerged as ambiguous as truth itself in the Age of Turamali. Regardless, Aunt Jen created a respected legal practice entwined with —for lack of a better descriptor— Turamali Spirit.

Cali found her Aunt Jen curious and enigmatic. When paired with Uncle Cy, she found the couple held a quiet power uniquely all their own. Cali often found herself at their home where she marveled at their end-of-workday stories. By the time Cali was ten or twelve, Sage and Bayani knew if she wasn't cavorting with her mare, Sabino, she was with Aunt Jen and Uncle Cy.

In the same hushed tone held with Kalen, Jen whispered to Cali. "A BioBot designed to improve, stabilize individual ethos, emotion … is it possible? Has what the public been told true? And, what happened today … to our ethos, *the* Ethos? Your mother is as troubled as you are Cali."

Gently holding both of Cali's hands, Jen studied the teen's face for reaction. "You're a budding rebel. Daughter like mother. But, Cal, can you promise to come to me? Whether you believe you need my legal advice or not?"

Jen added in thought transference, *Plotting simmers with you. Gather facts. Don't assume. Cali Cal, make wise choices from a place of inner knowing and conviction, without fear or anger.*

Cali shook loose from Jen's gentle hand-holding and whispered in frustration. "It's the letting go of anger and fear that's difficult. They drive conviction."

In response to Cali's adamance, Jen merely looked sideways and stifled a laugh. "Need I say more?"

In deference to the day's fatigue, Cali let out a childlike huff and shook her head. Point well taken.

As Cali and Aunt Jen held a special connection, so did Kalen and Aunt Kehl. Detecting Kalen's weariness, Kehlani pulled him to a nearby sofa where they sat, each other's adjacent knee jostling the other's. Kehlani's boho ankle-length dress took on a smudge of rusty brown from Kalen's jeans.

Kehlani pressed a palm-sized, polished, green tourmaline crystal into Kalen's left hand. In natural response, he curled his fingers around the famous crystal. Aunt Kehlani's voice was melodious. "Allow it to fill your soul tonight, smoothing rough edges, releasing tension ... This stone will open you to revelations tonight ... to nuances and the unspoken."

Soft Native American flute music drifted into Kalen's awareness, but where did it ...? Where was he now? Breeze from an open window skimmed across the gathering. A mix of earthy desert scent and Aunt Kehl's natural fragrance, combined with crystal energy and sound made Kalen lightheaded. As if suddenly given permission, Kalen allowed his defenses to fall succumbing to Aunt Kehlani's spell. Enveloped in her aura and feeling weightless, he floated.

Aunt Kehl's shiny reddish-brown hair ran in waves down her back and across the front of her bohemian style dress. Tonight, there was no usual long braid. As she gently caressed the hands of her spiritual son, two small stone bracelets stacked on her wrist jostled and glistened.

Kalen allowed his shoulders to slump, and just as Cali had done, he leaned forward and rested his head on his Aunt Kehlani's shoulder. In response, she put her hand in the middle of his back. *This crystal is much like the one I gave your mother years ago. Carry it with you.*

Grasping the sleeve of her dress with his free hand, Kalen held on to his aunt with fervor, as if she were the person to save him from the day's disturbing, discombobulating events. Their work with crystals yielded a special bond, much like Cali's bond with Aunt Jen. Kehlani spun magic that only an Adept could do for her sweet Kalen.

Sage and Bayani looked on as their teens were entranced by the physical and psychic touch of their aunts. As it should be. Biologic parents can't do it all, cannot be it all. They knew their children loved them, needed them, but it was difficult to witness the ever-so-gradual letting go of their mom and dad role.

Too powerful to be unfelt, grace and spellbinding magic emanated from the living room, momentarily relieving Sage and Bayani of their tension and fatigue from the evening's turmoil.

Jake and Cyprus, too, took in the vibrational shift. Sipping on beverages meant to relax, Jake and Cyprus spoke in low tones as they stood adjacent to the tiled kitchen countertop. Aware but unconcerned of the interactions around them. *Sensing* enough but not fully *knowing*.

A stiff breeze wafted through the paired patio doors mysteriously disrupting the spell. Kalen and Kehlani turned toward Cali and Jen who remained locked in telepathic discourse. Kalen stood and nudged his sister's arm.

"Cal, let's shower and get the trail off. Those dust rivulets across your cheeks are not doing your complexion any favors," he cajoled.

As he proceeded with his sister to the other end of the hacienda, Kalen nodded directly at their parents. *Give us a few to clean up. We're starving, and then we're ready for conversation.*

By all rights, Bayani should have slipped into shower mode as well. However, he knew if he did, he might not leave the confines of his warm comforting bedroom to discuss haboobs and BioBots. Helping the injured and frightened animals near the ranch and then riding out to rescue the teens had taken every bit of Bayani's remarkable strength. He had washed his face, rinsed his hair cowboy-style, and changed his shirt. Good enough for now.

Before the night quieted for anyone in the casa, both biological hunger and discovery about the tumultuous event had to be addressed urgently. Sage reached for Bayani, and they joined Cy and Jake in their conversation.

Feeling a need to continue intimate dialogue, Kehlani and Jen seated themselves across from one another in the living room. Kehl reached out for Jen placing both hands on Jen's knees. In seconds, Kehlani took in her dear friend's vibe and smiled crookedly at Jen.

Wow, you have taken on Turamali Telepathy with a vengeance! It's good, Jen. Cali needs you and Cy. Her parents are ports in a storm, while you and Cy are inconspicuous mentors and confidantes as Cali figures out her rebellious passion ... especially with this next wave of BioBots.

Sage picked up on Kehlani's telepathy with Jen. So, the twins do confide in the fireside amigos — things that Bayani and I may not know or hear. Another letting go. Yet, I know the twins will need more than their father and mother to get through what is coming with EthosBot.

Sage and Bayani, Kehlani and Jake, and Jen and Cyprus began building their own taco delights when the twins wandered into the kitchen, all scrubbed and fresh.

Cut just below shoulder length, Cali's caramel hair was slightly wavy and damp from the shower, framing her face with simple ease. The sun naturally lightened her hair, but in her teen years, Cali had played with natural essences to foster highlights and trendy streaks. Her hair and skin tone mirrored her mother's, even her desire to streak her hair color to make a statement.

In his physique, Kalen carried his father's Hispanic heritage. Kalen's hair was a dark natural brown, wavy mop dusting his forehead and ears. Sometimes, he wore it trimmed up and stylish. Other times as now, he simply enjoyed the longer length so he could run his hands through it and toss it around for emphasis. A bit of male drama with the hair counted. His seventeen years allowed for a tidy light beard that outlined his facial structure.

Together, the twins were stunningly beautiful. Clearly, they carried the genes of their parents. Their skin tone was tan intermixed with olive, and the deepness was seasonal or sunshine dependent. The Radiance BioBot ensured smooth flawless complexions that, combined with simple youth, glowed. At present, their countenances were flaccid revealing the day's wear and fatigue.

Jake was relaying the latest ranger story about how the wild animals fared the day's tumultuous sandstorm. He was both flabbergasted and provoked. He knew there were injured animals the rangers and wildlife vets had not gotten to, simply because there were so many miles to cover. As darkness fell, they listened, and when they heard no cries of pain or whimpers, they'd decided they'd done the best they could until daylight returned. The stampede had also caused wide swaths of brush and trees to be ruthlessly trampled.

His beloved open space, public land, and lifeforms violated in minutes by an unseen force. Jake's typical even temperament simmered. At least those who knew him felt it.

Instinctively and encouragingly, Bayani shifted his plate

to the opposite hand giving Jake a couple of light slaps on the back. *The animal suffering ... rips our hearts. Jake, don't let it break you.*

Jake stiffened. Not because of Bayani's sincere consolation, but because he knew Bayani's wife, Sage, had to be in the middle of something smoldering at *TIA* — some new-fangled bot to meddle in the existence of life. For Jake, the affectionate years of camaraderie and parenting the twins as the fireside amigos had steadily shifted to suspicion and discomfort, as word of the new EthosBot trickled through the media.

Even as the Radiance and Assault BioBots grew in scope and impact, he wondered where nature fit. Natural nature. Where had it gone? Or was he being nostalgic, not appreciating the benefits of biotechnology gone wild to save all from certain demise?

"Bayani ..." Jake whispered. "The bot thing again. This, this has pushed me today." After studying Bayani, Jake glanced at Sage realizing she knew, she heard. Bayani felt conflicted about uttering another word or telepathed thought.

Remorsefully, Sage interjected with her thought transference, *To be revealed tonight. I see the havoc of my work, this new bot. I hear you, Jake.*

Compassion, sadness, and confusion filled Sage. Attempting to find courage, she instead projected an air of stoicism and moved across the kitchen alone. Bayani and Jake looked at one another knowingly and moved in unison toward the wide-open double patio doors.

Electing to leave the teens to their ruminations, the adults wandered outside to the patio table and bench to enjoy companionship and sustenance. At least for the moment, it felt right, with the amigos moving effortlessly in unity as if this temporary separation from the teens was agreed upon.

In the kitchen, Kalen poured two glasses of fruit-infused water and handed one to Cali. They threaded their way past the outlay of food, building tacos as they went. They immediately plopped themselves down at the living room coffee table, placing drink and plate adjacent to their mother's current novel and then pillows beneath them on the tile floor. Either cross-legged or one knee bent upward and leaning against the coffee table, they silently dug in.

Cougar spoke. *Smaller animals were trampled. The young of herds and packs were severely injured. Sage … you know what needs to be done.*

Unable to admit or commit to action to the four-leggeds, Sage merely froze.

In a sudden spasm, Bayani dropped his plate. Of course, it was the Adept equestrian who, after rescuing animals and teens for hours, was fitfully taken by thought transference from the wild desertscape. Hearing *Cougar* target Sage in a message to the fireside amigos was the final overwhelm of the late day's events. Bayani grabbed at the buttons of his shirt as he slowly leaned on the table's edge.

Cougar, your companions … I'll be out later with the barn hands to check on those in our care. I hear you, Cougar and Coyote … not just tonight … and not only the words.

Chapter 3

ETHOSBOT

A mesmerizing warmth overcame Bayani, as Sage and Kehlani rushed to his side with each placing an arm around his shoulder or waist. Kehlani's intense auric field surrounded the threesome as she relieved tension and pain. Succumbing to the skills of two Adepts in minutes, Bayani recovered from the imploring four-legged telepathic message.

Stepping off the patio and into the desert, Kehlani and Jake held hands meandering several yards beneath the stars. Instinctively, Riley and Willow, Kehlani's beloved canine companions, strode by the couple's side. Mere feet away nestled in desert brush, *Coyote* and *Cougar* sent a further concise missive.

As the four-leggeds plotted tactically for the freedom of the confined long ago, so now we conspire with like-minded humans to end Ethos and its havoc.

With the relationship established at the outset of Turamali Telepathy, *Coyote* and *Cougar* communicated effortlessly with human Adepts and canine companions. Tonight's conversation was cathartic with noted intention and determination. All life honored.

As quickly as *Coyote* and *Cougar* had convened with the foursome, they retreated to open desert moving into the quiet dark of night. Riley and Willow followed Kehlani and Jake back to the warmth of the patio gathering.

Under Jake's fire-building skills, the patio's fireplace now exuded a robust pinyon fire with occasional sparks and wisps of floating embers. Abutting the adobe kiva exterior, a screen stood atop stone pavers keeping the embers contained. The earthy desert scent not only filled the yard but filtered past the double patio doors to the main living area.

The fireside amigos spoke in low tones about the day's events. Soon however, the conversation turned light as the longtime confidantes chose to reminisce about past adventures.

Inside the casa, Cali and Kalen had just taken empty plates to the kitchen and retrieved beverage refills when their parental crew strolled from the patio to the main living area. Each took up a spot on a chair or sofa, the wide arm of a loveseat, or comfy floor cushion.

Bayani had barely let himself sink in thankful rest into the sofa's cushions, when Sage pushed away from her perch on the arm of the sofa adjacent to him and strode across a few tiles. The impending account of events demanded that she speak as a restless professor in front of eager students.

Her braid of youth long gone, she fiddled with a few strands of her barely shoulder-length, shaggy style. The varying lengths filled out her face as she'd become more slender over time. Her light brown golden locks were now infused with natural graying streaks that, on Sage, gave her an aura of authority unencumbered by mainstream thought or dictum. The sleeves of her favorite sweater were pushed up to her elbows meaning she had something of import to relay. Catching candle and lamp light, her beaded bracelets and amulet necklace glistened as she fidgeted. Hung from a leather cord as a pendant, the watermelon tourmaline amulet was gifted by Kehlani years ago and worn perpetually.

Pacing, Sage began the narrative eagerly awaited by her extended family. "We've known for centuries that geomagnetism creates the world we know. When the field is disrupted by emissions from the sun or even manmade structures, the alteration in currents can be minimal and we adapt. Or as today, they can significantly impact the function of biological life and our engineered wonders such as our devices.

"Broadly, the afternoon tempest was a geomagnetic storm. They normally develop when the Earth's magnetosphere is disrupted by solar shock waves or coronal mass ejections. In essence, our roiling burning sun ejects rogue energy flares, and every so often, these flares are nasty. The flares are highly charged currents which disrupt natural and manmade electromagnetic fields (EMFs). Manmade energy fields include power grids and any communication that relies on satellites or air waves.

"Thus, it is no surprise the oddly generated geomagnetic currents today garbled or negated thought transference and hindered the electrophysiology of brain, heart, muscle ... affecting phototransduction for sight, the transmutation of sound to hearing ... in essence wreaking havoc with our neurobiology. Honestly, the storm impacted any electro-physiologic-based process in some manner, whether it was felt or not. In this case, it not only impacted the physiology of human and animal, but it also sparked scattered fires and created seismic waves."

Sage paused her nervous hair twirling and faced the intent family audience. "Even prior to BioBots, an index was devised to measure geomagnetic disturbances. It's known as the global Kp index, and it ranges from zero to nine with nine representing the most intense storm. At an index of seven or eight, a third or more of satellites become dysfunctional." Sage scanned the faces she loved. Everyone is so intent, holding on to every word I utter.

"Mom," Cali whispered. "What was the Kp index today?"

"It … it was locally … somewhere about an eight. That's what engineers and meteorologists informed us."

"Mom, an eight on a scale up to nine? It wasn't just pelting sand particles obscuring vision and hearing. Our entire electrophysiology was thrown off! That's why we were so disoriented too. We had heart flutter, and our muscles went weak … as in totally limp, weak while on our horses. We're lucky *they* didn't stumble or stagger! Poor Sabino and Kona were affected just as much as we were, and yet they took care of us. And Zaner was thrown from Desperado." Cali allowed pent up anger to tumble out in a jumble of thoughts.

"It was Ethos. Right?" Kalen probed. "It wasn't just a solar flare. This was Ethos. It was a localized Earth event. The solar flare may have affected various geographical locales, but here it combined with Ethos or crystal energy with devastating effects." Kalen's face was drawn as he now stared at his mother for an answer.

Sage nervously ran her fingers across her lips. She placed a hand on her chest and breathed in deeply but shakily. With shoulders slumping, she absently thought transferred. *What have I done at TIA? The ones I love were in peril today.*

As if on command, a series of brisk breezes blew across the living space bringing with it the sharp fragrance of burning pinyon. The pungent scent of damp creosote snuck in too. An isolated rain shower in the desert tonight? *Odd*, telepathed some unguardedly. Except for the tempest, the day had been nearly cloudless.

Sage began again with a whisper, "Indeed. Why such mayhem here in this pocket of the Southwest? There is more to it." She sighed heavily and shook her head in disbelief.

"It seems our work in biomagnetic medicine was purposefully targeted to create an isolated event. In the immediate hours after the Earth event, the Team Leads were pulled together to develop a working theory. There's agreement inside *TIA* that *someone* using a device, synchronized a predicted solar flare with electromagnetic fields and our cache of crystals creating an uncanny tempest. Corporate executives want to believe it was accidental, but Team Leads — all our internal experts — unanimously concur it had to have been orchestrated, planned. It was purposefully set off."

Not waiting for the dire significance of being 'purposefully set off' to stir outrage, Sage sidetracked into safe haven knowledge. "The science behind what occurred today is real. For instance, the Great Pyramids can resonate by concentrating electromagnetic energy. So, it's possible to fabricate a device to concentrate multiple energy sources and send it outward. Combine a solar shock wave with normal electromagnetic fields and the potential energy of our crystals and ... you could have exactly what occurred today."

Kalen spoke up to rationalize what his mother just postulated. "All crystals used in clinical applications undergo atomic structural change when subjected to temperature or pressure variation ... and thus create polarity and voltage or current to repair tissue and annihilate pathogens.

"… Mom, are you saying that minerals used in BioBot research and production were somehow synchronized with a solar flare to generate the intense energy field? Or was it EthosBot, because it functions differently than previous bots? … Furthermore, since we don't have any pyramids around here, it would require a sophisticated system to capture and direct solar, crystal, and our area's electromagnetic field to generate the sandstorm and seismic waves we experienced. And, who … *who* would know how … *how* to do such a thing and *why*?"

Kalen often worked with Kehlani when she led telepathy sessions for those in need of support to control thought transference in their daily lives. Over the years, Kalen had become quite astute in crystallography and human electrophysiology. Now, Kalen's incredible insight caused the group to stir uneasily.

Aghast and holding back no longer, Cyprus stood. Unable to suppress fury, he paced. "This wasn't a spontaneous event? Some nefarious entity plotted and pulled this off without our discovery? Using some sort of device?" He undid his man bun, and then fiddled it back into a messy wad at the base of his head. His typical steady hands trembled.

Uncharacteristically rattled, Cy processed the situation aloud. "A team of agents arrived at *TIA* within minutes of the … shall we say geomagnetic storm? Media chatter debates the executives' ambiguous statement of the event. People are speculating how the electrified storm transpired under the high security conditions of the biotech company. And now, there's a device and likely an inside culprit. The integrity of the investigation is already a muddy mess."

Local federal agents were always near *TuramaliScape*. Since the original eco-bot launch, the eyes of the world were forever turned toward the private biotech firm known for creating biologics and intelligent life, and healing Crystal BioBots. The government needed to be prepared for international and domestic nefarious activity. Better yet, the government had to anticipate and thwart.

Jake joined Cy in a brief pace. Then crossing his arms in front of his chest, he leaned against one of the skip-peeled poles separating living room from kitchen. Jake harbored his own fear and anger about the impact of newly created bots on the ecosystem under his jurisdiction and the land he loved so dearly.

Nervously, Sage pressed her fist to her tense lips. Secretly, she pondered. Rogue engineers, subversives within the company plot to dismantle the very work they helped create. It's worse though. These renegades create the pretense that *TIA's* biotech somehow spontaneously upends energy fields fabricating Earth events with great impact ... when indeed they've engineered something of great import to merely garner attention.

Under pressure and fatigue, Sage slipped accidently into telepathic mode. *I don't know exactly who they are, but what they've created is worse than Ethos.*

Every eye turned to Sage. Did they hear her correctly?

Who are 'they'? Do you know who was behind the sandstorm? ... What mysterious device has been created?

Sage held up her hands in a stop signal and shook her head in dismay. "I can't ... don't ..."

Heavy silence was pervasive. Seconds screamed to be counted.

Breaking free of restrained aggravation again, Cyprus spoke. "Sage, you knew and didn't inform me?"

More pointedly, Cy was equally irate and offended. Nearly twenty years of friendship and intense bot drama had sowed deep trust among the fireside amigos and especially between Sage and Agent Cyprus ... but where was trust now?

Cut to the quick by Cy's meaningful and painful query, Sage became unsteady. Had she indeed betrayed trust with Cy, by not informing him of whatever inklings came her way? Or had she simply been evasive, not wanting to face the harsh reality of the EthosBot and the turbulent undercurrent of employee unrest?

Suddenly, she could not carry on with the instructive narrative she planned. Trancelike, she moved stiffly seeking the comfort of her longtime love. Bayani welcomed Sage to the sofa as she settled fully next to him. Curiously, her streaks of gray hair now appeared more evident.

Cy, bot-teamers vent, bemoan, agonize constantly these days. Ethos trials have been a mixed bag. I hear, I'm aware, but some bot-teamers are equally skilled at hiding intent and action.

"Cy, was I to bring water cooler talk to you?"

Sage spoke aloud what she could, and telepathed what she couldn't.

Desperately tamping down interrogation mode, Cy placed both hands on the arm of the sofa breathing within inches of the top of Sage's head. Then he whispered, "What they've created is *worse* than Ethos. And you were going to tell me this when?"

Breath was suspended in the room. If others discerned the whisper, it didn't matter. Tone and action held piercing implication. Closest to the highly charged interaction, Bayani merely froze as he sat snugged against the eco-savior of yore.

Sage twisted her lips and blinked as tears rolled down her cheeks. "I'm so tired, Cy. Worn. All the Team Leads. We feel as if we're being crushed. Sorry. So very sorry."

Standing upright, Cy remained at the side of the sofa still within inches of Sage. "The FSPA is ever-present at *TIA*. Worse, you couldn't share your intel and warn me? Ill-founded supposition regarding water cooler conversation isn't going to help. Or better put, withholding intel from those who *can* help is outright negligent."

"Cy," Jen gently interjected. "Let her speak to what she knows. She's sharing insider detail, what the corporate execs are saying, doing. The rest ... what is suspected ... take it offline with her, away from this group." Jen could speak to his Agent demeanor as no one else could.

Sighing heavily, Jen continued. "Kehl, you've sealed us off? From telepathic eavesdropping? I think we all assumed, but this merits certainty."

"Correct. The hacienda is covered. Telepathic transmissions are blocked beyond these walls. Well, more concisely, verbal conversation and thought transference are muddled. No Adept, Hyperintelligent, or Insight can decipher our discussion. They can suspect, but it ends there.

"Also, you must know already but it bears repeating. Our animal Adepts know, hear ... even what we may not. They knew even before ... so when it happened ... still, all they could do is run ..." Kehlani trailed off.

To say more would make Jake angrier and Cali weep. Why she had strayed with the last clarification about human versus animal telepathy, she didn't know. The night was feeling increasingly strange even for Kehlani.

Cali harbored distrust and fear about the EthosBot. Despite revelations thus far, she knew there was more to tell. Persisting, Cali encouraged her mother to reveal more.

"Mom, just tell us what you can. How is Ethos different? Why would someone conjure a tempest resulting in tragedy? My friends and I were ambushed today by geomagnetic crystal enhanced craziness … we never even knew possible. We were sickened. Pelted by sand and wind until we couldn't see, hear, or think. Zaner … our horses, the animals, the cries, the pain … were terrifying.

"We couldn't communicate with you! Where were you? Our telepathy didn't get through. There's so much more to tell. You know that!" Unstoppable tears ran down Cali's face as her tirade escalated. With unabashed theatrics, frustration and fear were vented in the safe walls of home.

Kalen reached around his sister's shoulders, gently shaking her in consolation. *Let it go, Cal. You've said your piece. Now, find your peace.*

In response, Cali slouched against her brother. From Agent Uncle Cy to daughter-mother drama. Over a bot, a BioBot and a weirdly triggered sandstorm.

In the brief conversational pause, Jake felt compelled to elaborate on what Cali articulated so honestly.

"Cali's right. This EthosBot or fangled device that worked with it … didn't just affect mental health as the public campaigns promoting it profess. It blasted across the Southwest. We don't even know how far yet. The stampede, the fear, injuries … I worked alongside wildlife veterinarians and anyone who could lend a hand to save those in pain, or mercifully put to rest creatures we couldn't save. People. We don't' even know yet how many humans were injured. News media will tell us soon enough …"

Waving his arm, Jake continued, "There's a huge swath of land that suddenly appears clearcut. How long will it take for the land to be restored? The animals, plant life … intended or not, the impact on the ecosystem is gut-wrenching."

His voice faded and he rubbed his scruffy beard. He wanted to say more, but with Sage's face so drawn, he could tell more tears and surrender were near.

Sage wanted to run. Years ago, she felt this way — when she felt trapped in her underground hideaway after the unsanctioned eco-bot launch, and when authorities surrounded her on the *TIA* campus. Who or what did she want to run from now? Her daughter, Cy, Jake? Herself? The EthosBot and *TIA*?

"I've ... we've gone too far with this BioBot. I'm sorry, so very sorry for what happened today." Looking directly at Cali and then Jake, she whispered, "I didn't mean to be flippant in the science or irreverent to those who suffered today.

"Some of us suspect. But we can't ... we don't want to throw out accusations without evidence."

Cyprus had gradually backed away from Sage and the sofa as soon as she'd begun her apology. In one last dig, note of anger, or simply in agent mode, he telepathed so all heard his response to Sage. *We need your suspects, any intel you have. Leave collecting evidence to my team.*

Bayani rubbed his face. What a mess, he thought. "Here's how I see it. We've got all kinds of bots, crystals, and energy fields ... and they're tied up in creating what happened today. Perhaps it's worthwhile to refresh all of us about the mechanics of Crystal BioBots. Sort out how the original bots are different than Ethos. Then, tell us anything more about the intense sandstorm we just lived through."

"Agree," Jake stated. "Since we're back to the science of it, let's go through it."

Bayani's and Jake's comments restored some degree of calm and took the focus off Sage.

"Mom," Kalen began, "how about I explain the basics of the original bots, and you pick up with Ethos? Fill in anything I miss." Kalen perceived weariness from his mother. This was a simple way he could support her. With a nod and smile from his mother, Kalen plunged in.

"The original bot was the eco-bot. It was a skillfully crafted synthetic DNA virus designed to attach to plant receptors to rejuvenate botanical life. The virus was delivered via a hovercraft which was powered by the tourmaline crystal. With the right pressure of the craft, the crystal changed shape creating piezoelectric power.

"Botanical life was revitalized with unanticipated exuberance. When humans and animals consumed genetically altered plants and crops, they too became the recipients of health and vitality. Within weeks, the phenomenon of telepathy developed. It was believed the consumption of turamali virus-infused food interacted with neurotransmitters synthesized in the gastrointestinal tract, which in turn affected the psychoactive receptors of synaptic nerve membranes in the brain. The phenomenon was variable though, producing hallucination for some, hyperintelligence for others, and a whole range of telepathic abilities." Kalen paused.

"Earth's life was restored, even oceanic. Over time, we witnessed spontaneous intelligent biologic crafting by organisms to thrive in ecosystems now bestowed with new dynamics. Interestingly, as time went on, the role of the revitalization gene of the virus was forgotten or never clearly understood by the masses. *TIA* early on converted tourmaline to turamali — its very own intellectually protected name for the biologic and intelligent life it created. So, it was no wonder that people simply tied turamali and crystals to healing. Then, after communities near the mines in Asia had signs of being cured of some of the worst diseases with ingestion of homemade micro-crushed crystals, *TIA* pursued crystal-based nanobots." Kalen sighed and nudged Cali. *Your turn at this?*

"It's important what Kalen pointed out about the turamali virus. In an effort to control the wildly successful botanical effects across the globe, a few renditions of the virus were developed. The modified virus tempered effects, but after revelations from *Mission: Turamali* in Asia, all bot development shifted to healing and curing — humans, then animals. That is, healing with crystals alone. Although to this day, no one knows how the ingested turamali virus from crops and water permanently affected all of life. However, it seemed not to matter, as crystal therapy alone suddenly became the go-to and cure-all.

"Super metallic crystals were pursued with a vengeance as they could provide the perfect polarity, matching normal bio-electro-magnetic physiologic processes, but with a precise goal to heal. The Radiance BioBot was initially composed of tourmaline or quartz with the amazing capacity to heal millions worldwide with arthritis and back pain. It was an orthopedic bonanza.

"The Assault1 BioBot used crystals such as rhodochrosite which took advantage of iron, manganese, zinc, and copper. This bot took out parasites such as malaria and other insect-vectored diseases. *TIA* created an entire series of Assault bots to take out other pathogens.

"Despite general physical health and the demise of the old healthcare paradigm, anxiety and depression remained problematic. After all, shifting to a paradigm of health and Turamali Telepathy meant former ways of living and earning income were … well, no longer viable for many in healthcare and related professions. Life was kinda turned upside down for many. Physical health was great, but what do you do when you have no work, no meaning to the day? Within a few short years, the last frontier of healing was mental health."

"Cal, Kalen, you nailed it. Which brings us back to Ethos." Sage sighed heavily.

"The goal was to heal anxiety and depression. After all, Crystal BioBots — the Radiance and Assault versions — all targeted physical illnesses and pathogens that caused disease. But, what about mental and emotional stability? There was no bot developed to treat mental illness, to create emotional wellbeing. And there was nothing to shape or improve telepathy skills other than working with an Adept such as Kehlani.

"We needed a bot to target the very essence of how the brain creates thought, emotion, and mental state. The challenge, though, is that altering mental state can inevitably morph individual character and disposition. Directly interfering with synaptic transmissions meant inevitable consequential persona modification — with unknown risks that none of the Team Leads were willing to accept. At least early on.

"Yet, that's what this whole Turamali Telepathy thing has been about. Turamali directly impacted thought over time by a process we knew so little about. It was unintended. The botanical revitalization gene, transmitted by the virus, should not have had any crossover effect to brain signaling. Yet it did.

"So, we debated with C-suite executives and medical experts. Afraid to create a bot targeted at brain function, and equally fearful that if we didn't pursue it, some other entity would. Better to be in our hands." Before continuing, Sage ran her hands through her hair.

"EthosBot. First, we discovered that a single crystal vibration or mineral structure, as is used in the Radiance and Assault bots, was not a one-crystal-type-fits-all to heal mental states. The premise of emotional healing is as unique as every individual. When a stone is quietly grasped in the palm of the hand, each person feels the crystal's vibration differently, ranging from nearly painful to nothing. People are often drawn to a stone's energy if they intrinsically need it. Early on, we discovered a Crystal BioBot needs to be matched with the individual to achieve mental health. Hence, one of the reasons this bot has taken years to develop.

"Then, we identified a natural biomagnetic process affecting sight, mood, and even choice of crystal. Normally present in the retina of the eye and specific regions of the brain, cryptochrome perceives or responds to magnetic fields in a person's environment by generating electrical signals. It translates signals from a crystal, a mountain, a highly spiritual locale, or a man-made EMF into a physiologic reaction, a positive or negative feeling. We believed cryptochrome was an avenue to treating mental illness.

"Thus, EthosBot came into being ... ethos, meaning spirit or character of a group, culture, or era ... encompassing mood, aspiration, motivation ... a bot to create positive healthy ethos in the individual ... healthy ethos in millions worldwide. A subcutaneous BioBot in the hand, arm, or shoulder sends continuous signals to neurons thus providing mental stability and health. For trial volunteers, this became extraordinary, personalized crystal-healing medicine."

As if in response and on cue, a coyote pack yipped, snapping the assembled group's attention to the immediate, the tangible, the surrounding desert ... from bots and neurotransmitters to the simple rhythm of desert life. The wood fire scent continued to drift through the casa, temporarily easing breath and tension. The coyote pack trotted closer with more yips and howls. Perhaps, they wanted in on the conversation.

Cyprus picked up a short pace across the tile floor. "Historical footnote on BioBots noted. Sage, now bring us up to speed on solar and electromagnetic energy and how it's being wielded. There must be a backstory that I've forgotten."

Squinting her eyes, Sage looked thoughtfully posing the query, "Do you remember the geophysicist, Hailey Emir, who worked in tandem with the meteorologist, Dalton Malan, to determine why some of the original eco-bots failed in flight? Their findings eventually became public knowledge along with turamali-spread prediction models." Seeing nods from around the living room, she continued.

"It was at the end of that field investigation that Hailey mentioned the possibility of wielding EMFs to amplify, refine, or weaken the effects of turamali. Initial findings were difficult to reconcile. Both EMF and seismography readings were off the charts elevated. The electrical field in that locale should have been incompatible with life; yet life was unusually abundant compared to other bot-impacted areas. But there were also strange areas of die-off. Hailey reminded us that EMFs induce alterations in the human nervous system, and even cause cell mutations and death."

Agitated by the memory and current implications, Sage fidgeted adjacent to Bayani and wished her last words could be retracted. She prayed no one would address potential aftereffects of today's irrationally fabricated sandstorm.

"Once we began harnessing the natural energy capabilities of crystals, it was an easy ah-ha moment to realize inherent Earth electromagnetism, irrespective of source, could be paired with the normal electrophysiology of life-forms ... to alter, heal, wield at will.

"As the clinical trials with volunteers slowly advanced,

outlandish water cooler talk festered. Could local EMFs be harnessed to augment crystal therapy? Engage geographical locales where spiritual ley lines create sensational energy vortices? Somehow mobilize the sun's energy or solar flares? The synching of various energies was mind-boggling. Create a sort of walking, talking, telepathizing human with an embedded bot that harnesses surrounding energies ... resulting in lifelong anxiety relief ... forever mental stability and contentment."

With the last description, Sage let out a strained laugh. Every day she lived the science, but now in a state of overwhelm and fatigue, perhaps the science had a comical angle. Nonetheless, she hoped her attentive listeners grasped the connection between harnessing energy sources and bot development.

Several knitted their eyebrows, while some offered a crooked smile and then quickly shook off the weird depiction of a human transmuting energy fields as they moved about their day — all to attain a state of forever happiness. Due to an embedded bot!

Blinking nervously, Sage continued, attempting to bring the narrative back to what happened.

"Today's geomagnetic tempest appeared to be an unexplained intermingling of a solar shock wave and local energy fields which melded ... by virtue of EthosBot prototypes ... to create the electrified sandstorm. Anyway, what possibly happened is that someone — an intern has been the suggested scapegoat — mistakenly engaged a robust set of crystals of high polarity. Part of the EcoSphere II was blown out transmitting the force field energy waves across the desert — probably up to fifty miles or more."

With fervor and cynicism, Jen quickly interjected. "So, the company line is the tempest was accidental, created by an employee or intern. But not accidental because a predicted solar occurrence was synchronized with local EMFs and bot crystals? Something or someone pooled energy sources setting off the event."

Hearing Jen so impassioned outside a courtroom made Cy raise an eyebrow and smile at her, despite the gravity of the situation.

Defensively, Sage shot back, "Jen, your summation, although inherently ridiculous with contradiction, is accurate. Accurate enough."

Cy peered closely at Sage. In measured fashion, he repositioned his hands on the armrest where Sage sat and whispered at face level, "Synchronized. By whom and how? How, Sage? Combining those energies would require elaborate technology and capability to result in today's storm. I am not interested in the company's scapegoat, postulated coverup, or contrived messy R&D to hide the truth."

Unlike his typical agent self, Cy felt unhinged by the details being ferreted out tonight. He tried not to intimidate Sage with the same force of presence over her as earlier, but his last query about who and how likely agitated equally as much.

On top of Jen's inquisition, Cy's renewed persistence further unnerved Sage causing her to bend slightly forward and press her hand against her stomach. In visible angst, she rubbed her forehead and twisted her hands directly telepathing only Cy and Jen. After all, Jen was bound by lawyerly confidentiality, and at this point, Jen was pulled into this debacle in a way she'd not foreseen ... and Sage knew it.

There is a device. Rogue engineers. Others. Plotting. Plotting that is strongly cloaked. It's aggravating, but that's all I can uncover.

Slowly, Cy pulled back and stepped away from Sage. *We'll meet tomorrow. With Jen in tow if need be.*

All observed Sage's torment and some wondered how to console. Others still had anger to convey.

"Mom, after today, after what we went through … does *TIA* still plan to unleash the EthosBot?" Cali demanded to know. "Mystery device and creepily synched force fields aside … this bot is unlike any other BioBot. Impacting the essence of what we feel, who we are. It's more than just a fix for mental illness. A bot specific for mental health with ramifications across lifeforms we cannot possibly anticipate! And what about the four-leggeds, the seafaring creatures? What impact will the EthosBot have on them? No one talks about that. … Like Zane and the rest of us today, we became victims of Ethos without even having the darn bot implanted.

"But turamali and bots are never just about what the teams at *Turamali Innovative Arts* believe them to be. The world has been forever altered. We likely would not have *TuramaliScape* and communes whose mission it is to work with galactic beings. Turamali has not only expanded our mode of communication, but it has already altered what we believe and choose. It's not just biologics and intelligent life and medical nanobots. It's *interference* with life … with who we are … from microscopic algae to coyote to human. Mom, I need to be heard! The voices of *Coyote* and *Cougar* must be heard and heeded. Your turamali escapade saved two decades ago, but enough already. No more. Let us be."

Over the course of the evening, Cali's demeanor shifted from accusatory to instructional to philosophical. Now, it was a daughter telling her mother what should and should not be … social, economic, political ramifications of bots … and a personal cease-and-desist demand … hitting home.

Watching and hearing her daughter in the context of the evening's onslaught against her, Sage suddenly felt suspended in time and space. Sage felt lifted — an out-of-body experience? She saw Cali, but instead perceived her own childhood photographs when she was a teen. The resemblance in facial expression and demeanor was overwhelming. *It's me again. Cali is me.*

Defenses down, Sage telepathed without regard to those present. *Reflection of myself in my daughter, my Cali. Every facial feature, every bit of spit and vigor. The Rebel. We share the same eyes. The same Rebel vision. The me that crept across the star lit desert night to stealthily launch eco-bots meant to save Earth.*

Sage put her hand to her mouth. Disbelief. *Reflections of me. Seen before but not like this.* Sage let out a sob and bit her lip to hold back the emotion. Lost in ethereal mayhem, she slumped against Bayani dropping her face into her hands. Instinctively, Bayani shifted sideways to hold her.

Too, Kehlani wanted to dart over to Sage to console, but she held back. It was deeply emotional for Sage and thus for others. Feeling compelled to reach out, Kehl telepathed, *Sage, hold the amulet.*

In slow motion, Sage reached for the amulet around her neck and held it tightly. The watermelon tourmaline felt solid in her grasp sending a vibration to her inner core. With that sensation, she knew her Cali was right on the mark. Sage wept with abandon.

Cali swallowed hard and rubbed her face, finally looking at her mother in astonishment. *Childhood stories of the Rebel were always about you. You were the Rebel. Not someone else.*

Conflicted between her mother's spiritual insight and her own fury, Cali fiddled nervously with her hair and stood. Now, Cali was the one to feel like running. She saw Jake put his drink down and look reassuringly at her. Instinctively, Cali stepped into Uncle Jake's embrace. In a smooth fatherly fashion, Cali was pulled into a much-needed hug by her uncle as the two shared trepidation.

With a shiver, Sage felt the night's chill seep into the living space despite Bayani's warmth. Emotionally heavy discussion had stirred buried memories. Sage felt lost. *B, need you.*

Bayani telepathed, *Sage, where did you drift to? I'm right here, holding you. Cali is a reflection. You've known that, but tonight you see it.*

After several minutes, Sage faced her children and companions.

"Cali ... Cali's not so far off."

Gathering composure, Sage breathed deeply. "Her ethical point is well-taken. Is it our place to wield control, even if our intention is improving mental health like we've tackled so many other physical illnesses? No one debated the ethics of rehabilitating arthritis and broken bones, nor of curing disease. But tinkering with mental capacities ... even as turamali seeds hyperintelligence but also creates false perception. Is it ethical to intentionally fiddle with neuron signaling and the process of manifestation in the brain? Telepathy was happenstance but Ethos is intentional."

With hands on his hips, then restlessly tenting index fingers across his lips, Cyprus sought to clarify the readiness of Ethos for mainstream launch. "Your teams at *TIA* have played at this science for years now, with resources continually redirected to new versions of the Radiance and Assault BioBots. Up until today, we felt confident there was no threat from the EthosBot.

"Honestly, our biggest effort has been monitoring for

corrupt action — internal, domestic, international, or even galactic interference — to pilfer the technology in whatever stage it was postulated to be. Fortunately, from the agency's viewpoint, the BioBots targeting physical disease have taken center stage. The EthosBot remains in clinical trial limbo with the model still tossed about in intellectual circles — at least publicly."

Cy raised his eyebrows. "That is until today." He studied Sage for a reaction but only saw renewed hair twirling.

Carefully enunciating each word, Cy continued. "Now, Sage, the wicked stir and wonder ... what is *TIA* up to with the rumored EthosBot and a strange haboob wreaking havoc?"

Sage pulled the sleeves of her sweater from elbow to wrist. She nestled closer to Bayani purposefully scooching her upper body up against him. The repercussions of the event sinking deeper into her psyche, she trembled and spoke to the new reveal.

"Cy is right to be concerned about the message that emanated loud and clear today from *TIA*. The C-suite executives were chasing down media demands about the disaster even before we could assess what occurred."

Sitting forward, Sage rubbed her thighs. "I'm dreading tomorrow. Cy, we're going to need support from authorities just to enter the campus."

Cyprus paced towards Jake and Cali who still leaned together against the wood pillar, and then around the seated companions. "How did I end up surrounded by the highest Adepts and more bot catastrophe and drama?" Cy could feel it coming again. Déjà vu.

Sensing Jake's need to speak, Cali released her arms surrounding his waist and lifted her head away from his shoulder. Jake cleared his throat and tenderly held Cali's forearm in a quick caress, as he pushed away from her and the pine support column. He anxiously rubbed his chin and eyes fell on Jake. His torn, tattered, and partially bloody ranger shirt had been replaced after rescuing wildlife. Perhaps he should have worn it here tonight to make a point.

Now, he stood across from Sage, with only his demeanor betraying the day's trauma. Jake tilted his head, assessing Sage and wondering how much more she would reveal to her closest companions tonight.

"Sage, is the EthosBot human-ready for worldwide distribution? Do practitioners have protocols for subcutaneous use? You've done volunteer trials, and there are prototypes. Is there a scheduled launch? What more is at risk here?"

Sage glanced at Cyprus whose seconds-ago exasperation turned to a serious stare.

Her silence encouraged Jake to persist, unafraid to offend any friendship if that's what this conversation entailed.

"My god, Sage, it wasn't just your own children and their friends hurt today ... although that could have been far worse. What will be reported in the news tomorrow about others residing or working in the affected area? ... Wildlife frightened, disoriented, trampling their own young. I saw the agony."

Jake looked to Bayani as he knew that he and the ranch hands had been inundated by equine casualties and small animal injuries. Being Bayani, he had simply focused every ounce of energy on managing the crisis with barn staff, neighbors, and nearby veterinarians. For Bayani, there had been no time to point fingers or jaw about the mechanics behind the event. There was barely enough time and help to do what needed to be done to alleviate immediate pain. Then, the posse was put together to get their teens home safely.

Somberly, Bayani nodded at Jake while rubbing Sage's knee. Betwixt, Bayani thought.

"Sage, large swaths of open range land were devastated. That hinders the availability of food for the animals who did survive this crisis. We also suspect that natural water sources have been disrupted by the consequential seismographic waves. Whatever role Ethos has … falsely incriminated or not … it's still rampant bots and … runaway energy synched with bots." Jake breathed out letting his shoulders relax. *As your daughter so adroitly and vehemently did, I too have said my piece.*

Yet again, with tears pooling around her eyes, Sage rubbed her thighs. By now, her face was blotchy, and her hair disheveled from twirling and running her hands through locks of hair.

For once, Bayani did not know how to continue consoling her. The situation had fully spent his energy and ability to sort through the right and wrong of what his lifelong partner was doing at *TIA*. Unlike the former debacle of the turamali eco-bot, the EthosBot had weighed heavily on him from the outset.

"Jake," Sage whimpered, "Again, I am deeply apologetic. I haven't had time to assimilate all that's transpired. You're right to be infuriated. All the questions about the status of the bot … impending use and what risks remain before it's formally launched are apropos. I just don't … I don't know how to answer that. Even the powers-that-be likely remain at wits end, at a loss for answers."

Sage buried her face in her hands again. Then rocking forward to a standing position, she exclaimed, "I apologize to all of you, my dear family and fireside amigos. As a Team Lead on the project, I could have, should have done more. More to examine the rationale and soundness of tampering with what we are calling the human ethos. I should have pressed our corporate executives for better accountability as we ventured into development."

Exhausted and ashamed of letting down the people she loved, Sage picked up Magic burying her nose in the terrier's wavy coat. Time for four-legged consolation. The human companions were justified in outrage and disappointment. Within seconds, Marley, Riley, and Willow too surrounded Sage where she sat. The gentle canine souls offered temporary comfort.

Candlelight flickered and earth essences drifted throughout the room. The outside temperature was dropping providing both a refreshing breath and a shiver to some.

Kehlani *knowingly* whispered, "Indeed more than one, and there is a contraption."

Kehlani eyed Jen and expounded, "Precisely, a cadre of culprits. Whip-smart employees ... seething, conspiring. Pervasive inside *TIA*."

Jen tilted her head, "And they had intent and design. Device design, yes, but orchestrated intentional design of the tempest."

"This was no mistake," Kehl continued the synchronous discussion between her and Jen.

"Intent to bring ill-fated attention to the EthosBot. But was it to make an activist statement or to destroy?" Jen speculated. "Perhaps both — a shout-out to the world, as well as dismantling of the EcoSphere and all that's tested there."

Another heavy silence fell. Human dialogue, of any type, burned out. To seal the evening's end, whisper breezes carried the scent of smoldering wood fire from the patio. Uncannily, a light trail of smoke floated above the assembled portending more to come.

The evening's discourse was perceived. *Coyote heard* but was quiet.

Kehlani got up from her chair and stood next to Jake. Together, they turned slowly to see *Coyote* positioned between the still-open double patio doors. The others gazed at the open doorway. No one moved.

Coyote stood proudly with bold resolution. His fur was aglow, mottled in grays and shades of cocoa and sable. Golden brown eyes captivated and held human focus. The stare of a coyote encountered on a trail is unforgettable, but the stare of *Coyote* sears to the soul.

Without a sound, he was joined by two other pack mates. Unmoving, *Coyote* held the fixed gaze of the assembled a few seconds longer. Tonight, he sent a thought message to every soul in the casa.

The fireside amigos, Cali and Kalen *heard. The four-leggeds will not rest. Will not allow EthosBot to undermine wildlife, lifeforms. Concrete TuramaliScape is a tenuous façade.*

Then, he deftly trotted off with his mates. No one heard *Coyote* trot lightly into the desert. No one ever did.

Unbeknownst, Sabino, Kona, Dakota, Bandit, Desperado, and Defiance meandered off with *Coyote*. Kindred. They'd all been in the thick of it today and wanted no more of it.

Chapter 4

TRYST & SCHEME

"Spill, reveal," Zia nudged Kalen and Cali. "You both are privy to the darkest secrets ever about what caused the electrified haboob and stampede. We know your mom, Uncle Cy, ranger Jake, and the Adepts all had a say the night Zaner was thrown from Desperado. You've gotta tell us what you know so we can scheme our best."

Cali and Kalen had debated what to share with their fellow tryst & schemers. They knew they'd be pushed to tell all. They felt compelled to stick with the storyline being promulgated by *TIA*, just as their mother had explained — minus the notation that something worse than Ethos has been created able to bring multiple energy fields together and minus rogue insider plotting. The twins speculated their bright fellow schemers would probe and unravel the truth despite any of their intended omissions.

"Guys," Cali stalled and shook her head. "It's the same song and dance the media's reporting from the company. Someone or something set off highly polarized crystals in the EcoSphere II, and somehow it was timed with a predicted solar flare. Those energies combined with our surrounding electromagnetic fields resulting in everything we endured."

The couples were lying on serape blankets tossed to layer against the sandy earth and stray clumps of desert grass. Since leaving *TuramaliScape* classes at noon, the group had met up with Carson to sneak away to their favorite river tubing spot. It was a little-known, secluded stretch of rafting fun which the teens passed methodically on the way to and from classes. It was amazing that no one else had discovered the spot. Then again, it was uniquely situated near an equine trail that led from the hacienda to *T-Scape.*

This bit of adventure paradise had been owned by the hacienda years ago. With the construction of *TuramaliScape,* this modest adjacent parcel had been designated public land. In fact, it was technically under the state park and Uncle Jake's jurisdiction. Initially, the corporations had insisted they purchase the land outright, but in the end, compromise won, and public land use satisfied all parties.

After securing their horses at the downstream exit point, the group trudged upstream twice to glide down the river on rafts and in tubes. They would have gladly walked and made the river run twice more, but drying off in the warm sun next to their heartthrob and being lazy were far more attractive undertakings. Soon, warm autumn days would quickly turn too cold for this sort of escapade.

The concussion had kept Zane for two nights at *T-Care.* Although doctor's orders were for 'school only, no horse riding, take it easy for one week', Zane couldn't sit out while his dearest pals had fun. They reluctantly acquiesced to his salesmanship. They even saddled up his Paint, Desperado, for him. The negotiation resulted in an edict of 'everyone walks on their horse, trotting as-needed, no cantering/loping, and certainly no galloping'. It resulted in an easy trail ride where verbal bantering brought laughter. Now the gang of amigos — Cali and Carson, Kalen and Zia, and Zane and Nate — were engaged in plotting ... plotting to end the EthosBot and further tragic repercussions.

Turning first to stare down Kalen and then Cali, Zia scrunched her eyes at the twins. "You two know more. Someone or something set off the geomagnetic storm. Doesn't sound or feel accidental to me. Ethos is still at the heart of this tragedy and still needs to be stopped. Correct?"

"Z, yes, simply put, Ethos stirred a pot of solar and electromagnetic energies ... creating a big-time mess with our neurobiology, whipping up particles of air and sand, igniting fires, and causing seismic waves."

Considering how much more to say, Cali fiddled with a loose thread on the blanket. "Likely not accidental ... which is different than the current company line, so you guys ... you guys didn't hear this from me." Cali lightly hit the blanket in frustration and looked to her brother.

Kalen too felt compelled to say more to the schemers. He huffed out a breath returning a look of resignation to his sister. "Cali and I can only say so much. We can't jeopardize any of you. Besides, isn't it enough to know that Ethos remains a culprit?"

Adjacent to Kalen, Zia felt his unease. Although, much like her closest friend, Cali, she was determined to shut down whatever the heck caused the catastrophe they barely lived through.

Pushing discussion forward, Zia posed, "Ethos then ... how do we destroy the devious bots?"

From lying on his stomach perched on elbows, Kalen sat up on the serape. "Even if we figure out how to access the *TIA* corporate building, we'll still need access to the hidden recesses where the EthosBots are kept. In fact, we don't know where the BioBots are stored, so how long would we wander around the Art Studio and other locations to find them?"

The Art Studio of the biotech firm hosted the Biologics & Intelligent Life and Crystal BioBot Teams, where all great things were contemplated and developed. It was the core work area for those operating in biologics. The Technology Team, the hardware and software elite, were tucked away in their own space.

Kalen continued pondering aloud whether a heist and destruction of the EthosBot was practical and possible.

"We know prototypes are being tested in the EcoSphere, but we don't know where the crystals and bots are stored. Furthermore, some clinical-ready bot version is being used in human trials. We don't know how many volunteers, how many trials, nor if the experimental subcutaneous BioBots are still intact in people living among us."

Feeling a chill, Zia rolled to a seated position, pulled on her sweatshirt, and nestled the side of her body up against Kalen for warmth. Kalen leaned in and kissed her affectionately on the cheek. He momentarily gazed at her still damp, tousled wavy bob as it fell against her silky smooth complexion.

"Guys," Zia began, "we all believe the EthosBot is dangerous and needs to be stopped. But Kalen has a point — the mechanics of this might surpass our capability. Say we get inside and get to the devious little bots, then what? How do we destroy them? They're crystal activated. And how many are there? Worse, what if we miss some? It's not just the devious bots themselves, it's the technology and all the data stored intangibly in ethereal places. We'd have to locate every data bit and byte and delete it forever. I don't even know if deleting e-data is possible anymore."

Kalen burst out laughing jostling Zia. "What the heck is intangible data stored in ethereal places?" His laughter was contagious and soon the others chimed in teasing Zia.

Somewhat defensively, Zia shouted over the chortles, "Not funny, guys, and you get what I mean. I know you do. Does anyone else see the complexities of the scenario with me? ... Besides, the more I think about the seize-and-destroy mission, the spookier it makes me feel. I don't like it. Plus, my dad's a federal agent. He would throttle Zaner and me."

With the fading afternoon sun, the wind picked up. Cali, too, pulled on her sweatshirt, and since her jogger shorts turned-bathing-suit were dry, she yanked her riding jeans on. Better. She squirmed into a semi-cross-legged position and reseated herself as close as she could to Carson. In response, he smiled broadly at Cali and tossed his well-worn leather jacket across her shoulders hugging her into warmth which emanated easily from his lean, muscular frame. He was every bit of classic broad-shouldered handsome caballero.

With laughter subsiding, Cali knew Zia would push the dialogue back to serious. Considering the challenges of a seize-and-destroy mission, Cali eyed Zia and her brother.

"Z and Kalen, there are challenges here. No doubt about that. It comes down to how committed we are to stopping the EthosBot. And, I guess, to what degree we need to prevent further use. We could put a significant glitch in the development and production process thus far. Maybe we don't have to annihilate this precarious, devious bot. Perhaps we create enough havoc that the project is delayed for years. It comes down to how bad this bot could be once launched mainstream. Could what happened with the enhanced prototype happen again, or worse be usurped by a foreign entity and transformed to a truly evil purpose?" Cali tightened her lips and pushed locks of hair behind her ear.

Unwinding his arm from around Cali, Carson straightened his back and leaned forward with his hands flat out in front of him on the serape. The stance put the companions on notice. Something was stirring with the senior member of the gang.

Carson gazed at Kalen and Zia, then Zane and Nate. "This is monumental, my fellow schemers." Then he pivoted toward Cali with the words, "This. This is far different than Sage Amaris, your mother, creeping into the old *Turamali Innovative Arts* one moonlit night to launch a handful of eco-bots to save botanical life."

He paused, adjusting his focus back to the entire group. "From my vantage, we're in an entirely different place now. A seize-and-destroy mission is possible but only if we garner inside assistance. The security built into *TIA* is formidable. But, convincing someone on the inside or finding a sympathetic employee would give us access."

Kalen and Zia squinted their eyes and nodded.

Kalen telepathed Cali, *Our fellow schemers are too smart. They already suspect the Earth event was purposeful by rogue insiders.*

Cali had no time to respond to her brother when others chimed in.

"After the geomagnetic storm, you can bet there are sympathizers inside the company who want to work with us." Nate played into the idea of finding employees equally irate and amenable to action.

Zane nearly shouted, "Outright activists. Inside and outside *TIA*. Read social postings."

Carson smiled at the enthusiasm. He held up a hand indicating he had more to say.

"Then to Zia's point — how do we destroy Ethos and

data? At least enough of it, that we derail future trials and the plan for mainstream use … essentially what Cali referred to. In fact, Cali may have hit on an alternate strategy to achieve our goal."

Waiting for signals from the group, Carson sighed. "Guys, we simply create enough chaos without even entering *TIA* or physically destroying the devious little bots."

"Social chaos," Zia murmured. "Overthrow it from the outside. I'm so in!"

Whispering to Carson but unabashedly fine with her friends hearing, Cali nuzzled his cheek. "You're so frustratingly right most of the time. Smart too … It's why I love you …" As she brushed her lips across Carson's face, she took in his scent of woodsmoke and leather. For such an earth-centered way of life at the ranch, Carson was highly educated and a thinker.

"Hey, we should articulate our goal. If we're not going to enter *TIA* and seize-and-destroy bots, and instead create social chaos, we need to define what that means … what it involves. I know, I'm irritating and too rational, but stating the goal is important for agreeing on our mutual action." Nate fingered stylish glasses on the bridge of his nose and then absently rubbed his designer stubble beard. "Clearly, succinctly. Something we all agree on. Then we can drive strategy to reach that outcome."

Spoken in a teacher-esque manner, Nate could be endearingly irritating. However, Nate was Zane's close friend. A few years ago, they'd met at a summer camp where Zane ended up teaching Nate to climb trees, sail, and ride horses, while Nate guided Zane through wizardy-techie camper experiences. If opposites attracted, this condition was met. The two had become inseparable — which was fine for Nate's parents but not so much for Zane's. Zane's dad was a federal agent with a stereotypical officer demeanor and stodginess even in the enlightened Age of Turamali. Nate was a year older than Zane, and his parents lived by the *Turamali Life Festival,* old-style Woodstock, hippie motto of embrace crystal harmony, respect lifeforms, transcend, be free ... it's a love-in time.

Zane was the first to lightly slap his forehead, "Good frickin' grief, man. We're not in school." Then the laughter started up again rippling across the group.

Familiar with being teased, Nate slumped and smiled but still stood his ground. Seeking to gear up confidence, he rubbed his five o'clock shadow again with the back of his hand.

"Okay, look. Is the mission to disrupt the EthosBot? Its production or use? Alter the BioBot, so it's harmless or simply dial back the potential? Disengage this ill-defined mechanism that creates geomagnetic sandstorms? Get sympathetic insiders to destroy it entirely? The goal easily makes a difference in our tack — whether we still bust into the concrete fortress, disrupt the technology remotely, or create vehement social doubt and resistance about the nature of EthosBot.

"And as a side note to the mission of choice, busting into a concrete fortress likely comes with jail time, even if some misdirected employee provides access ... versus fomenting social debate that, at worst, results in awkward publicity and family ostracization for us, but is notably devoid of felony charges."

Acknowledging the soundness of Nate's discourse, Zane looked sideways at his confidante with a crooked smile. Neither was sure of what they had going on with the other, but this much was true — the friendship and respect ran deep, and they enjoyed being together. Sometimes, they felt like misfits with the romantic couples, and at other times, they felt right at home. Thankfully, the tryst & scheme amigos didn't judge.

"Disrupt versus destroy ... busting into a concrete fortress ... jail time or social ostracization ... heavy thoughts ..." Zia laughed and sighed, not sure what to feel.

"No search, seize, and destroy mission? Mom would be much happier if we didn't take that tack!" Cali breathed a sigh of relief. "Up until this point, I assumed we'd need to bust into *TIA*. Perhaps there are other ways I hadn't considered. The geomagnetic storm incident has me heck-bent on physically annihilating the devious bots, as Zia loves to call them. Perhaps disrupting passive consent and tolerance of the Ethos biotechnology is a better path."

Then murmuring, Cali added, "Too, attacking the merits of Ethos takes out that part of the equation that generated the tempest, as well as the unknown mind-bending of Ethos itself. Tinkering with neurons has never sat well with us, especially when we still know so little about how turamali and the virus spun telepathy."

"So, gang, what should our stated mission be to thwart the little demon?" Zia persisted, wanting to bring some closure before packing up the river rafting playdate. Those who hadn't shrugged into dry warm clothing now did so.

"Disrupting the technology would mean preventing access to at least some of the necessary components to produce Ethos. Complicated but possible." Kalen looked around at his companions. "For now, we avoid disrupting the technology per se. Instead, we discredit the BioBot, cast doubt, sow fear," Kalen stated with certainty.

He leaned forward as if to nail the go-forward edict. "If we do this, then society alters the course of the EthosBot through public sentiment and resistance. We already have the storm, stampede, and EMF disruption as evidence of what this technology is capable of wreaking. We spread the word this new spin on biotech could translate into our worst nightmare ... that Ethos is not only geared to impact the who-we-are aspect of our brain but can combine with other energy fields to wreak mayhem. Fear is palpable now, so we foment, keep that sensation alive, truly making Ethos the evil bot we know it to be."

Cali fed off her brother's words. "The goal is to avert the EthosBot launch into mainstream use by turning society against it ... which in turn stalls further development and production, and hopefully, disables current bots, so we don't have a rerun of bot-amplified tragedies. We persuade and plant seeds of mistrust in the EthosBot's ability to heal emotional afflictions. Quite simply, we instigate social upheaval against Ethos."

Zane snapped his fingers. "We turn healthcare and mental health experts against the wicked bot. Surely, there are some who observed trial results they didn't like. And still others who believe this project should never have been undertaken. They've probably been silenced. We need to find the experts who feel as we do."

Surprised at Zane's insight, Nate added, "The trial volunteers ... I wonder if any of them had negative effects from the experimental EthosBot? There must be some. I don't know how we'd find them."

"But we don't have to find them," Zane countered. "Once we get social media buzzing, the disgruntled, maligned, frightened trial volunteers will come to us with stories."

"They'd probably turn up anonymously though," Nate replied. "I'm certain they all signed confidentiality agreements that are pretty tight, with negative repercussions clearly delineated should they violate the terms."

"But once the tide of public opinion turns, anonymous stories are fine," Kalen concurred. "We'll have sentiment and others in positions of power who can stall or put an end to the EthosBot project."

"Turn world view, social mindset against Ethos. I like it." Zia smirked, grabbed Kalen's hand and raised it in a victory signal.

Carson nodded and shifted from sitting to kneeling back on his heels. "Now, we need a project name. A name we can use so if others hear it, they won't know to what we are referring. Then, we need a list of strategies, and who is going to do what. This could be a long haul. Compared to a seize-and-destroy mission, bending collective thought takes time. Likely could take twists and turns we can't anticipate or may not be prepared to handle. We must be ready to accept risk. For one thing, social contacts, media posts, and whatever else we do could be traced directly to us. We'd be labeled instigators ... usurpers of BioBots which have been perceived as health saviors really ... until now." Caron considered his companions. "This should not be lightly undertaken."

"Consequences different than jail time, but nonetheless could be life-altering for each of us depending on if we're discovered ... or not, hopefully." Cali paused. "Once we start seemingly innocent threads of dialogue and debate, it could take off like a firestorm."

Nate jostled Zane whispering, "We can handle not being discovered in the electronic communication world ..."

Cali heard Nate's comment, but she remained lost in thought about potential repercussions of their plotted social action. She rubbed her mouth.

"My gosh. Do you think we could stir up enough

concern and fear that our concrete *T-Scape* could be in jeopardy? *TuramaliScape* is also a significant university and residential community, and we don't want mishap or violence coming to anyone residing there."

Cali recalled *Coyote's* message about *TuramaliScape* being a tenuous façade. *Could we be accused of anarchy? Is social disruption a criminal offense? We know history, but what about now in the Age of Turamali?* Tentative to verbalize a worst-case scenario with ill-defined risks, Cali telepathed to those cavorting with her.

Either in discomfort from the speculation of potential consequences or from the growing autumn chill, Zia visibly shook. In sweet response, Kalen rubbed his hands around Z's shoulders and arms trying to generate warmth. He reached for his fleece riding vest and zippered her into it, ending the effort with a soft kiss.

Kalen then studied his sister. She was stubbornly adamant about putting an end to EthosBot. Her moral compass was so much like mom's. Like their mother, Cali would take the risk. Perhaps more than others seated riverside. In fact, his sister might even put her welfare on the line, especially if it meant saving her fellow tryst & schemers.

Adding to the communal mindset, Kalen sighed heavily. "Bending social sentiment beats breaking into the *Turamali Innovative Arts* fortress. The media is already ablaze with heart-wrenching stories involving humans and animals. We add fuel to the fire. Thus, we need to plot our strategy carefully ... what we'll say, every nuance, and through which media and influential experts."

Suddenly, Zane laid back on the blanket. "This is huge, guys, and I'm quite frankly spent. Plus, I'm hungry. Our afternoon food supplies are gone. People with recent concussions need sustenance or they hallucinate." Smiling playfully, Zane thrummed his fingers on the blanket.

Responding with good-natured groans and giggles, the six companions decided it was time to pack it up and head back to the hacienda. River tubing equipment and blankets were rolled up and secured to equine companions. They bid farewell to the secluded adventure spot. Since it was Friday late afternoon, there would be time to mingle, snuggle, and poke at one another over a firepit-inspired dinner.

♦

Dusk descended on the trail riders as they approached the hacienda. *Sensing* the couples' arrival, Bayani telepathed to Cali and Kalen.

Did you hit the river? Well, you must be hungry. I've got the crew stirring up the firepits and my famous tamales. Don't worry ... The adults are headed to Jake and Kehlani's casa tonight. The ranch hands will take care of you.

Thanks, Dad, for giving us space and trusting us. Kalen replied before Cali had a chance to do so.

By the time the trail riders strolled up to the barn, Bayani and Sage were gone leaving the barn hands to help untack the horses. Of course, each rider took care of their own steed and riding gear, but it was always appreciated when the ranchers wanted to help with the tedium of untacking, cleaning gear, brushing down and settling each horse.

Two of the ranch hands tended the fires as well as the fire-roasted tamales, kettles of rice, beans, and churros nestled in foil — Southwestern cowboy-cowgirl essential delights. The wafting scent of cooking food made stomachs yearn. Soon, the ranchers and teens shared the feast. They made their plates, and each group settled around their chosen firepit talking and laughing only when their mouths weren't full.

Carson had initially taken his plate and joined the ranchers. After all, he was the associate hacienda manager and believed camaraderie was fundamental to everyday work relationships. After nearly an hour of recreating with the ranch hands, he grabbed several churros and joined the teens.

Cali visibly brightened and shyly smiled as Carson approached with the sugary cinnamon treats. He distributed a churro to each one with shouts approving dessert time. Then kissing Cali on the side of her head, he sat snuggly against her on one of the ranch's outdoor loveseats.

"Good timing, honey. We're tossing about project names. We need your ideas and vote."

"What have you got so far?" Carson scanned his gaze around the semicircle.

Kalen and Zia had snagged the other rattan loveseat, and Zane and Nate lounged with their long legs extended from overstuffed chairs. Facing Cali and Carson, the others shouted their ideas while laughing and poking fun at the names each didn't like.

"Dust Devil, Devious, Tempest ... Crazy Paint, Sanity ... Mind Field or Minefield."

Listening to the suggestions, Carson joined in the laughter. Then he pumped one of his free hands in a downward motion and whispered just loud enough to be heard over the crackle and spark of fire. "Guys, we need to keep it down. I could hear some of the conversation over at the other firepit. Remember, covert op here."

Responding in a determined whisper, Zia voted. "I like Devious, of course. Fits the little evil-doers purpose."

"Crazy Paint, for sure, after my mare who promptly propelled me into a tree during the storm!" Making a comical gibe at the horse he cared for, Zane smirked and waved his arm.

"Easy to remember," Kalen commented. "Crazy Paint has a nice ring to it. Anyone who hears it may believe we're training up Desperado. After all, we're equestrians, and Zane's Paint made a memorable statement."

"Mind Field or Minefield are really cool ideas," Nate spoke up. "I mean the double entendres are killer. Mind Field obviously related to what the EthosBot affects. Minefield as that's what we feel this bot is full of — explosive mines just lying in wait! Sanity is good too, but is it too closely linked to our target?"

Cali pushed forward slightly, leaning one hand on Carson's knee. "Mind Field and Minefield are great. They feel like tongue twisters though. I like Dust Devil, Tempest, and Sanity, but they may be too easily associated with the sandstorm and bot. Agree with Zia, too. Devious is short, sweet, apropos, and if others hear it, they may just believe errant teenagers are being teenagers."

"Dust Devil, Tempest, and Devious are solid. Easy to recall, to say." Carson chimed in after Cali. "But agree. Dust Devil and Tempest could quickly be associated with the sandstorm or Earth event … which is fine when we're posting or writing. However, we don't want to clue anyone listening, overhearing verbal or telepathic conversation. Devious is just plain cute." He turned and winked at Zia.

"So …" Kalen dragged out a conclusive tone, as he smirked at Carson for acknowledging his girlfriend's preferred moniker. "Project Crazy Paint or Devious are the least likely to garner suspicion or make a connection to the EthosBot. They both work. Crazy Paint because Zaner suffered from his mare's frightened response in the storm. None of us will forget that. Devious because what young adults would not dabble at being devious? It's built into our DNA."

Everyone laughed heartily. Full bellies, fun in the sun rafting fatigue, and the sincere warmth of genuine friendship placed an unusual, relaxed spin on the scheming. Scheming that, if they allowed themselves to consider in serious daylight, could cause pause rather than laughter.

"Yeah, I can go for Project Crazy Paint or even simply Project Paint. We can tell people we're plotting to paint one of the boring *T-Scape* concrete façades with a tantalizing mural fit to stir debate over the good, the bad and ugly of our world." With a bit of a sneer, Zia made her point, then after a sigh added. "Goodbye to Devious. At least as a formal name. I'll concede." Then she gave a sideways smile to her companions, with a particular blush as she looked at Carson.

Cali caught the poking and gazing between Carson and Zia. Who could miss it? The tryst & schemers were comfortable in their current pairings. Jealousy was not a thing. For now. Still, Cali abruptly ribbed Carson with her elbow.

"Vote?" Cali queried. Seeing nods, she tossed out the most recent suggestion. It was unanimous. Project Crazy Paint was now official.

Serenity settled among the schemers. Pinyon embers emanated heat and a familiar consoling scent. The ranchers had dispersed a few moments ago, after removing the food and kettles and ensuring the firepits were safe. The night felt suddenly whole and poetic. The couples gazed upward at the star-frosted Milky Way as it arced and swirled across the dark sky.

The evening temperature hovered near fifty degrees, but the fires had deceivingly kept the nearby air quite warm until now. A breeze gave Cali a quick shiver, and Carson instinctively pulled her closer. Kalen turned his knees inward toward Zia running his hand delicately through her hair. The couples whispered. Should they remain under the stars or head inside for intimate cuddles?

Feeling particularly spent and slightly lightheaded from the laughter, Zane leaned sideways on Nate's shoulder and instinctively held on to his friend's forearm for stability. The *T-Care* professional had warned the concussion would take a toll for several more days, possibly a few weeks. It was now evident to Zane that perhaps he had overdone it today. Nate placed his hand on top of Zane's, gave a quick squeeze of support, and slumped further down in the overstuffed chair.

Cali jostled Carson's leg and pushed off toward Zane and Nate. Seeing them with their eyes closed gave her pause about disturbing their peaceful brotherly-like pose. Carson stood too, folded the serape on the rattan loveseat and joined Cali.

"Zaner, Nate," Cali murmured as she crouched between their outstretched legs. "Guys, it's getting chilly. Zaner, I'm concerned about you. Saw you nodding off a few times. Despite whatever Radiance BioBot variant they gave you, the concussion is taking a toll."

Zane reluctantly tried to focus on Cali. She jostled Zane's leg again. "We shouldn't have let you plead your way out of following doctor's orders. The trail ride and tubing were a lot for you. You barely debated naming the project."

She paused and looked up at Carson who took up the conversation. "Guys, you're welcome to crash at my casita. I've got a guest room. Just let your folks know that it got late, and well, you are struggling some. I can see it."

"Think it's a good idea," Nate chimed in. "I'm in university living at *T-Scape* now anyway, so my folks aren't an issue. Hey buddy, what do ya say? Let's meander over to Carson's casita and get you comfortable."

Zane mumbled short phrases about his father being inflexible and bureaucratic, but when Zane stood to leave, he had to grab Nate to steady himself. "Just a little dizzy, guys." Decision made.

As Carson helped Nate with Zane toward the casita, Carson gave a shout. "Kalen, Zia, you can hang out too. I've got room. Mi casa, su casa." He gave a quick laugh with the last comment.

"Thanks, but Zia and I are going to enjoy the night sky, and then likely head up to the main casa."

Acknowledging Kalen and Z's alternate plan, Carson gave a nod and salute with his free arm.

Kalen, be careful. Mom and Dad will be back soon. Cali promptly messaged her brother.

I know. But if we fall asleep on the living room sofa, Dad won't say anything. Mom will simply give me her troubled look in the morning. And, what about you staying at Carson's? Now that's ... Cali, you are the one who should be careful. Dad will be upset.

Wanting so very much to be her own person in every minute and live life her way, by her choices, Cali shook her head and blurted, "Kalen, we're almost eighteen. If they find you and Zia cuddled asleep in the living room, they'll know I'm with Carson. They ... they can come find me."

My Cali is trouble, Carson telepathed without forethought.

Babe, I'll take the hit from my parents if it comes to that. Tonight, I'm staying with you.

Now, Carson guarded his thoughts. This hacienda is my life. I love it here, and I'm good at what I do. Bayani loves the business acumen I bring plus rapport with fellow ranchers. I don't want to give Bayani a reason to let me go … because I'm having a tryst with his daughter.

Within a half hour, Carson and Cali had Zane and Nate settled in the guest room of Carson's casita. Zane thought messaged his parents, and the response had been expectedly terse. Regardless of mixed parental approval, Zane smoothly fell onto the bed, grateful to be fully reclined.

After ensuring his pal would rest easy, Nate nestled on the well-worn leather sofa positioned beneath the guest room window. He pulled a Navajo blanket up to his chest and scrunched the soft fabric pillow under his head.

Cali and Carson plodded around his kitchen for glasses of water. With jackets off and skin now warmed by the heat of the casita, Carson pulled Cali in for a deep kiss. His muscular arms wrapped around her, and his hand slid up the back of her neck through her hair. Feeling the strength and pull of his body, she leaned into his chest and slid her hands beneath his untucked shirt. He responded similarly with her loose-fitting blouse.

When Carson's firm grip enveloped her bare skin, Cali shuddered and hesitated.

"Too fast?" Carson whispered as he pushed strands of her tousled hair back with the palm of one hand.

"No. Well, maybe. I love you so much and I want to be with you all the time. I know you want more. I want more. I'm so drawn to you with every fiber of my being." Cali pressed one hand against the middle of his chest while digging the other into his back toward her. Push and pull. "I'm scared, Carson. I don't … I haven't … god, I want you though!"

Carson smiled broadly and held Cali close while hands remained on bare vulnerable skin. "Honey, I want you, yes, in every way imaginable. But I'm in no hurry, and I will never rush you, never convince you of something I know you don't want or are frightened of. Sweetheart, we take our time."

Cali sighed heavily. It's one of the many reasons she loved this caballero. Patient to a fault while being unnervingly take-your-breath-away handsome and genuinely respectful.

♦

Bayani and Sage knocked on Carson's casita. It was after midnight. After returning home from the adults' night out at Kehlani and Jake's, Zane's parents had contacted them. Yes, Zane had told them where he'd be and why, but they still worried given Zane's recent fall from Desperado.

Bayani didn't want to create a ruckus. As hacienda manager, he had a duty to ensure the safety of staff. Plus, his daughter was missing from her bed, and he could guess where she might be. Bayani intended to give Carson an opportunity to come to the door. Sage tamped down her motherly instinct to rip inside and drag Cali out.

They'd left Kalen and Zia asleep in their living room. They appeared innocent enough and were soundly in slumberland.

Bayani waved the nano chip, which lay beneath the skin of the topside of his wrist across the door's handle. Sage and he proceeded tentatively inside.

"Carson? Cali?"

With no response, they quietly looked around. Within a minute, they found Cali cuddled with Carson on his bed. Both were fully clothed, nothing x-rated. Praise the Higher Powers.

Then they spied Zane and Nate in the guest room,

each soundly asleep and lightly snoring on their respective furniture. No concern here. Maybe it was a good idea for Zane to stay put if he was lightheaded. Perhaps it was a kind, mature action for Carson to take in these two for the night, rather than allowing the unsteady compromised hacienda guest to leave the property and take a chance getting home.

Perhaps not so wise for Zane to river tube and ride his horse against medical advice, but such was the mind of youth. The young adults could have done worse. They had fun.

Despite an innocent appearance, Carson taking Cali to his bed was not a professional action for the assistant manager. Cali had been warned and Carson knew better. Young risk-taking love.

Bayani, they scheme. I know they do. Ethos weighs heavily on their thoughts. Now, the trysting is blatant. Tryst & schemers. Our teens and our friend's teens ... guessing Carson and Nate are in on the scheming too. They've certainly all got the trysting down. Sage was irate.

Thinking and even *sensing* what the young amigos were up to was one thing, but seeing her daughter sleeping with Carson, and her son with Zia ...

Coyote yipped and caught Sage's attention. *What's important here?* She heard. She heard and the question entranced.

As they stood outside Carson's casita, Bayani pulled Sage into a bear hug. Then, he gently released her, cupped his hand around her neck and passionately kissed her — his lifelong partner, the one he fell in love with the moment she walked unannounced onto the ranch two decades ago, and then rode Sabino as if she'd ridden his mare a million times before ... so long ago and yet not.

Bayani rested his cheek and lips against Sage's face and whispered in her ear. "Tryst & schemers, yes, my sweet Sage. Cali and Kalen are perfect though. We pulled it off! The kids ... are ... perfect."

"We did, B. We did, and they are." Sage let Bayani swoop her up into his arms. Their tryst awaited.

Chapter 5

SPOOKED

The juxtaposition was remarkable but not unanticipated. Dotted with wispy clouds, the characteristic crisp Southwestern azure sky gave way to the sparkling cobalt river and waterfalls of *TuramaliScape*. Planted with design purpose, the natural beauty of succulents, cacti, shrubs, and trees was interspersed among the arced light gray concrete structures.

Emerald, olive, and forest greenery undulated with the morning wind. Lanky ocotillo swayed from the weight of bright red flower clusters at the very tips of tall spiny stems. In competition, nestled among dusty green leaves, deep purple Texas Ranger blossoms shouted.

Soothing landscape and captivating colors were suddenly jarred by the sight of a darkly painted mural. On a smooth concrete wall, facing the riverfront for easy visibility, a concise message was depicted.

In vermilion, 'End Ethos' lettering was several feet tall. Implying rough edges, the word 'End' was artistically jagged. In opposition, 'Ethos' was blunt and boxy with the letter "E" lying horizontally, suggesting a dead bug with the vertical lines. In fact, there appeared to be an unusually expert rendition of an insect nestled in the reclining 'E'. Human and animal charcoal figures dotted the image but were strategically smaller than the text. One had the immediate sense of being overpowered by the seemingly corrupt Ethos BioBot.

Comically, or perhaps not so funny or entertaining, several demonstrators were dressed in black as insects. On their backs, they attempted to mimic the dead 'E' on the mural. Alongside the painting, the gist of their act was spooky.

Chanting overcame the customary calm and sound of *TuramaliScape*. The easy rush of water over concrete structural form and function was drowned by a thousand or more activists. It was difficult to tell how many were leading the protest, as passersby joined out of adamant support, and still others seemed to join due to curiosity and sympathy departing when it suited their need.

Although shouts were various, the main chant was "BioBot Not!"

Messages on hoisted signs were creative and direct. 'Don't mess with my neurons!' 'Neurotransmitter this: RIP EthosB.' 'Anxious over Ethos Ethics.' 'Leave Mother Nature to her haboobs!' 'End Ethos!'

Finally, 'Assault the Ethos' was clearly a play on the other well-established and life-altering Assault series of BioBots which healed pathogen related conditions. However, it begged the query — did some believe an Assault Bot should be developed to singularly terminate the EthosBot? Interesting concept, but at present, BioBots attacked disease and healed. They did not attack one another. Still, the play on words was a jab at *TIA*.

Rather than compete with the morning's social unrest

and noise, *TIA* had set up a modest sound stage in the rambling, hilly interior of *T-Scape.* Trusting they would attract their own audience, *TIA* positioned the stage in one of the large parks. Much of the recreational space was surrounded by concrete residential structures, and thus, the goal was a muting of outside shouting and chanting.

In the past when they constructed something similar for a public announcement, *TIA* had referred to the space as their amphitheater. Since BioBots ruled health, no one questioned their possession of the amphitheater-like space. In reality, *TuramaliScape* was a global commercial and residential development with corporate ownership rights ending at respective structures. Assuming open space and surrounding parks were free for their corporate use was ostentatious — especially in light of the recent geomagnetic storm which was accordingly tied to the innovative EthosBot.

Gabi Breeze, *TIA's* public relations manager, fidgeted at the bronze hovercraft-inspired podium. Mimicking the wingspan of the original eco-bot craft, the top portion of the podium was broad and narrow at the base. Normally in her element, Gabi thrived during public appearances. Today, however, her eyes darted over the expanse of people assembled. She appeared to absently rub her neck, but then thought better of such a public gesture and instead brushed her hair back nonchalantly.

Trying to soothe her own fear for her daughter, Sage invited Cali to join her and hear the company's statement in-person rather than on a virtual screen. Sage believed the ambiance would provide an alternate perspective on the Ethos BioBot and give rational context for what had transpired only days ago. True, the BioBot had created unintended tragedy, but it also offered life-altering emotional stability if it could achieve robust clinical efficacy.

Little did Sage realize the activists had grown in number and voice on the *T-Scape* campus, and to boot, had a blatant visual painted across a concrete wall that had sprung up overnight. So much for a rational corporate climate to soothe her daughter's anger and abate rebellious action.

When Cali saw the threatening proclamation, she immediately telepathed to the schemers. *Remember the off-handed remark about Project Crazy Paint being a mural on a T-Scape concrete wall depicting the good, the bad, the ugly? Looks like we've got the bad on display. Too prophetic, Zia.*

Sage had simply hustled the two of them away from the scene. Recalling her own familiarity with social activism, she never caught the true reason for her own daughter's startled reaction to the 'End Ethos' painting. Sage thought Cali's reaction was more spooked than sympathetic to the cause. *Interesting* was all Sage could think at that moment.

To be honest, Sage agreed with Cali and their extended family. Despite cautious development, Ethos had progressed to the point where it portended devastating results rather than dependable, clinically reproducible emotional and mental healing. The recent environmental event could not be ignored without serious reconsideration of the Ethos project. The timing of the geomagnetic storm, due to an apparent action from inside the company, weighed heavily on her.

Sage had suspicions, but those involved were going to great lengths to hide their criminal efforts. Her thoughts rambled. Kehlani and Jen *sense* people with clear intent to undermine Ethos. Of late, I hear a multitude of voices. Rogue engineers. Are they the ones who synchronized force fields? Other insiders too, and there's dissension.

Finding a position close to the front of the stage, Sage's thoughts shifted to family. Cali stood next to her, but the distance between them was not inches between shoulders but a chasm. Despite the emotional rift, at least her daughter was standing adjacent.

Although Sage agreed with her daughter on the need to pause the EthosBot, she did not agree with the intended action Cali secretly harbored. Sage was an Adept. She could read her daughter. Sage respected Cali's privacy, but the intense emotion around Ethos was difficult to miss and scheming was evident. Tearful dialogue from a few nights ago still tugged at Sage.

"Welcome, everyone." Gabi Breeze haltingly began the prepared corporate statement. Designed to enliven and engage the audience, upbeat music faded but remained audible.

"As you know, the BioBots we develop heal life. The original mechanism was a bioengineered botanical virus meant to revitalize and revitalize it did. The eco-bot produced abundant food, and now, hunger no longer affects the world!"

Muted clapping caused Gabi to pause. With preassigned staff in the crowd to instigate timely cheering, she'd hoped for more enthusiasm. After all, the intent of this media campaign was to mitigate anger over the bizarre sandstorm by focusing attention on the successful history of the biotechnology.

"It soon became evident that super metallic crystals emit perfect electrical charges for physiologic integration and healing. Over the years, the series of Radiance BioBots have healed common painful conditions, and now bestow ultimate vitality worldwide."

Gabi raised her arms high to encourage audience exuberance. Although still sporadic and less than anticipated, audience applause caught on. Then, she continued the accolades.

"The Assault series has annihilated viral, bacterial and other infectious pathogens!"

Now, acknowledging triumph of the BioBots, Gabi was pumping a fist in the air. The cheering grew, but somehow felt exceedingly modest compared to reality — the cures and near pain-free life bestowed by *TIA's* biotechnology was astounding. Flummoxed by the muted audience engagement, Gabi simmered. People forget what life was like barely two decades ago.

Tempered enthusiasm was mixed with a sense of foreboding. Gabi Breeze felt it and forced a smile. After all, there was a virtual screen displaying her appearance and deportment, larger than life, as she delivered the speech.

"What occurs in the mind is also physical ... physiologic processes through which turamali forged telepathy and hyperintelligence. Building on the success of the Radiance and Assault BioBots, we turned our attention to healing emotional and mental afflictions. Thus, as you are aware, the EthosBot has been under development. It has been successfully trialed in volunteers with moderate and severe anxiety or depression, and for this, we are proud to have begun the journey in helping many."

Implying the many who were already saved by the EthosBot, Gabi waved an arm across the audience. With no applause, only restless stirring, she cleared her throat and wondered what happened to the audience-planted cheerleaders.

"Recently, an Earth event affected life within an undetermined radius of our campus. Initial investigation has revealed that an experimental Crystal BioBot was incorrectly tested inside the EcoSphere II.

"The consequential phenomenon and disruption of electromagnetic and seismic fields were unintended. At *TIA,* we hold ourselves to high standards and deeply regret the impact on all those who suffered. As have all of you, so too have we witnessed the media coverage of the tragic distress of both human and animal ..."

Suddenly, a megaphone blared, "End Ethos!" Along with the shout, streams of activists marched through open space toward the audience and stage.

Someone standing next to Cali shouted at Gabi, "Was it Ethos? Did the EthosBot cause the mayhem?"

Then others began yelling questions, apparent facts, and demands at the perplexed speaker.

"What experimental bot this time? We have a right to know what you're doing!"

"It was Ethos! The EthosBot killed my ..."

"You can't mess with our brains, our emotions!"

"Enough BioBots, enough! BioBot not!"

Gabi Breeze struggled to regain composure. Before she had an opportunity to respond and restore control, a tall security agent escorted her away.

As if the public relations manager being whisked away gave permission for the onslaught, the crowd of protesters quickly stormed the stage. As they did so, those in the audience were pushed and shoved forward, unable to retreat.

Sage tripped as bodies fell into her. Cali grabbed her mother's arm trying to keep them both upright. The air felt stifling.

With a jarring motion, Cali lost her balance. Both fell to their knees, just feet from the base of the stage. In the chaos, telepathic messaging was wild and incomprehensible. *Crushed.*

Then out of the tumult, they heard. *Go under. Under. Crawl.* Cali and Sage must have simultaneously heard Kehlani's thought transference, as they both turned toward one another, and together plunged forward with all their might.

Progress was excruciatingly slow as people continued to fall onto them, then pushing off ... only to be re-assaulted by another body. Someone would fall, scream, cry. Time and conscious thought were suspended as fighting for air and life took control.

As they army crawled beneath the heavy skirt of the stage, Cali felt sweat or blood trickle down her face. Once under the sturdy frame, both Cali and Sage rolled to a seated position cowering as thunderous noise surrounded them. Feet pounded above them. Knocking and slamming of objects hit the sides of the structure. Seeing others had made it safely beneath the stage too, they took account of their hiding spot.

"We need to get out of here, Mom. What if this structure doesn't hold?" Cali shouted to be heard.

"This could be the safest place for now. Until help comes. Security should be here." Sage tried to breathe deeply and found it quite painful. She shifted. *Now I know how Zane felt. Did I fracture ribs?*

Seeing her mother's pain, Cali responded, "Wait here. I'll crawl to the rear and see if there is open space, a way to get out."

It was only a few feet to the backside of the structure, but after the adrenaline rush and physical beating by the crowd, it felt laborious.

"Mom, mom! We can get out. Can you make it?" For the first time in her life, Cali worried about her. Within a minute, Sage had gone pale and weak.

Cali scooted back to her mother, and together they

pulled themselves out from under the rear of the stage. A few people raced by. As they stood unsteadily, a stiff breeze greeted them, filling their lungs and drying the mix of tears, sweat, and blood on their faces.

Someone in a uniform approached the pair placing his hands on each of their shoulders. Cali and Sage were escorted to an area where several Float emergency vehicles and staff were already busy assessing injuries.

Seated next to her mother and holding her hand, Cali cried. Her mother looked terrible, and Cali herself was scared. Others were on stretchers with crush injuries, while she spied two motionless forms beneath dark sheets. Overwhelmed by yet another bot-inspired incident, she began to shiver.

"Mom, Cali!" Kalen ran from his class on the *T-Scape* campus. After dodging among the wounded and vehicles, he finally found them. He barely had time to kneel in front of them when a medic informed the trio the two injured were being transported to the local *Turamali Care.*

"I don't need to go, but my mother does." Cali was adamant. With Kalen now here, she could go home with him. She simply wanted to escape the intense drama of the morning.

The medic placed his hand on Cali. "Look, you need stitches at the very least. Non-negotiable." He tilted Cali's head and pushed a section of bloodied hair aside. She winced. *This guy is cute and obviously good at his job. Guess I acquiesce.* Cali did not intend to telepath, but unguarded and compromised as she was, it slipped out.

The medic smiled and thought to himself. He'd gotten the cute comment before, but this time it felt like it meant something. You're the daughter of the famous Sage Amaris who secretly launched the original eco-bots. And, you both got caught up in today's brouhaha. Wonder if you and your mom were on opposing sides today ...

The medic snapped his attention back to the moment at hand. "Your mother needs to have the bruising around her rib cage evaluated. Blunt force trauma is nothing to mess with. We need to move." The medic looked at Kalen who nodded. "You can ride with them. We have a few other people already in the Float. Let's go."

The medic assisted Sage into a section with recliners, as she already had an intravenous solution engaged to prevent shock. Kalen guided Cali to a padded bench where the less severely injured and ambulatory were already lined up.

Upon arrival at *Turamali Care,* Bayani was standing outside the entrance with others anxious to know the status of their loved ones. His stance was wide with arms crossed tightly against his chest. *My girls. My leading ladies. As Uncle Cy says ... is there ever an end to this?*

Somehow, Sage had taken on more blunt force trauma than Cali. She had hairline rib fractures and bruises on her abdomen and legs, which made Bayani lightheaded to look at them.

Crystal healing or not, hematomas and the potential for hemarthrosis were present. Coagulopathy — albeit an obscure concept to Bayani — was real and could be life threatening, or so the medical staff attempted to explain. *T-Care* treated Sage for shock and pain, and of course, they gave her the recent Radiance8 BioBot — tourmaline perfected intervention for just this occasion. Sage's chest was wrapped to prevent further damage and support healing.

Although *T-Care* staff tried to persuade Sage to remain for one night, she stubbornly declined. Despite the enlightened age of medical care, being monitored and poked at in an unfamiliar room was frightening for Sage. It was yet another situation where she felt the need to run from and to the comfort of home.

The doctor said she was stable but precarious due to the extent of severe bruising. A strange summation from a physician, but the point was taken. Even though Bayani would rest easier with Sage under the watchful eye of *T-Care*, he chose not to fight the battle. Instead, he carefully listened to the discharge instructions.

Sage put her faith in the Radiance8, and with Bayani at her side, bid farewell to *T-Care*. They spotted Kalen and Cali lounging outside on manicured grass. Cali had quite the bandage affixed to the side of her head, but at least alongside her brother, she was smiling.

Bayani and Kalen assisted the wounded into the family's Float vehicle. Soon all were settled at the hacienda, with Magic and Marley nestled against those who needed them most.

Sage wanted to rest in the living room, and Bayani believed it was best there too, as the twins could look in on her. At least through the night, Sage was supposed to be monitored. The next twenty-four hours seemed to be the golden threshold that *T-Care* staff had insisted was the make-it-or-not point of homeostasis. Kalen said he would also look in on Cali a few times during the night, and that sat well with Bayani.

Before Cali adjourned to her bedroom, she plunked down on the coffee table and faced her mother.

"Mom, I know you wanted to share your world with me today. Funny, you thought I'd see a straight-up corporate side of things, and instead I got a glimpse of your past. The mayhem you stirred up with the original bot must have been a lot like today. Just want you to know I *see* you, Mom. I *hear* you. ... Sleep tight." Cali affectionately rubbed her mother's arm and gave her father a quick goodnight hug.

On the sofa, Bayani scooched next to Sage's elevated legs. He gently brushed her cheek. "I could have lost you today. That crowd surge turned deadly for some. Honey, we talked about this before. Is it time? The 'Rest in Peace Ethos' messaging is outright spooky. People are angry."

"Very soon, B, very soon. I'm making a change. Moving on. With you ..." Sage drifted to sleep.

Chapter 6

SPOOK

Schemers were at it.

Carson was missing, but he had ranch duties. Cali felt somewhat guilty for not missing him. She gazed down at her phone and the medic's contact details. After the injured were settled at *T-Care*, he approached Cali asking if he could leave his number with her. He hadn't been shy. His directness surprised but impressed her. *Gabe*. He carried a calm confidence. Perhaps it came from being a medic, or, what made him a good medic.

Cali had spent nearly the past year exclusively with Carson, and to have another guy show interest was flattering. *Gabe*. She felt drawn to him and wasn't sure why, especially since she was in love with Carson.

A meetup for a drink is harmless, she thought to herself. Besides, everyone needs acquaintances, pals — a variety of friends from all walks of life. It's been almost two weeks, so it won't appear that I was immediately enamored with him. He was darn cute, though, that's for certain. *Gabe*. The stitches and bruising on my scalp and forehead are nearly healed, so I don't look like roadkill anymore. Touching the tender area of her forehead, she sent Gabe a message.

"Cali! Yo, are you with us? Forget Carson for a few minutes and hang with us on Project Paint." Zia was frustrated. "Since the *T-Scape* riot, you keep zoning out on us."

Jokingly, Zia squinted her eyes at Cali and pestered, "Do we need to worry about you? Did you get a concussion or worse, and we just don't know about it?"

Cali blushed and rubbed her cheek in response to the heat she felt. Zia suddenly knew and glancing at Kalen, Zia realized Cali's brother knew too, or certainly suspected. The twins were close. Despite discretion and attempts at secrecy, the Age of Turamali Telepathy impacted the special twin connection intensifying claircognizance. As for Zia and Cali, they simply knew each other as only longtime best friends do. Clairsentience was ingrained.

Oblivious to the interchange, Zane and Nate were discussing Spook.

Ignoring his sister, Kalen cut in, "Zaner, Nate, update on Spook. How's it holding up for us?"

Spook was a software program developed by Zane and Nate. It had begun as a project at summer camp and then blossomed into what it was now. Spook rerouted and hid the source of Project Crazy Paint communications — in essence creating a trail of spooks. Every social post, every electronic message was untraceable. Originations and internet protocol addresses were 'spooked'.

Putting to work monikers they had originally considered for their project, they retained two as their cyber aliases. Zane and Nate were known as DustDevil, and Cali, Zia, and Kalen were known as the TripleTempest. The mechanical intricacies were simple, but also complex. Perhaps well-conceived or maybe not.

The DustDevil role focused on the ongoing functionality

of Spook as well as keeping nefarious interlopers at bay and summarizing social media metrics for the group. They didn't often need or want to contribute to blogging or dialogue. If Zane or Nate did, they were known as DustDevil@...

The TripleTempest was responsible for researching, developing posts, and engaging in conversation. Their task was so monumental, they had resorted to listing all their undertakings on an antique, discarded chalkboard. It was decent, prairie schoolhouse size, and the chalk meant they could erase damning evidence at any time. Although, locating the chalk to use on the board had been an undertaking unto its own. Thankfully, chalk on cement was still a thing for children and those with that artistic bent.

Acting as cyber sleuths and instigators, the TripleTempest culled through clinical trial data trying to identify experts and volunteers and the means to contact them, studied *TIA's* newsletters and broadcasts searching for ways to undermine the EthosBot, and stirred up heated debates about the ethics of Ethos and anger over the recent BioBot initiated Earth event. Monumental was an understated descriptor for the youth taking on the discrediting, disenfranchising, and general diss-ing of the EthosBot.

Cali, Kalen, and Zia all used the cyber alias, TripleTempest. If authorities investigated, there was no way to technically trace who composed what string. In truth though, tone and writing styles remained discriminators, and up until now, the three were able to discern which one of them said what — which was important when they were trying to build consensus about dialogue.

Indeed, the cyber aliases were simple but presented complexities. The final rationale for shared cyber monikers was shared responsibility, culpability, and deniability. They all did it, but who really did or said it? Wouldn't lawyers have a field day? Hopefully, it would never come to that.

The tryst & schemers usually met two or three times a week at Nate's hideaway located in his dormitory on campus. Being away at university had its perks. Furthermore, this university had carved out multiple rental spaces for students who wanted to develop their own business or pet project.

In synch with *TuramaliScape* architecture, the student residence was a concrete labyrinth of semi-circular living space, grand concrete staircases, towering atria, and skylights. On the top floor of the labyrinth, rooms were fashioned with daylight and egress windows, curvilinear concrete desks, and the same wireless technology throughout *T-Scape.* Squished full of notes and scribbles in various chalk colors, the old schoolhouse board sat awkwardly atop a concrete desk. Propped at the base by various small rocks, it leaned against the wall.

"Spook is perfection, my friends. Performing just as intended," Nate proudly stated.

Zane pushed back in his chair and elaborated. "Since it took time to plot and plan, we've only been posting about two weeks. Our followers are growing exponentially by the day."

Zane squinted turning unusually serious. He messed with his T-shirt rubbing his collar bone and shoulder. "We need to be careful. Already, tension is rising. We knew we'd build on the anger and fear surrounding the sandstorm and stampede, but there are calls for more action." Zane hunched forward, massaging his upper thighs.

"Your martial arts, Tai Chi taking a toll, bro?" Seeing his zany friend turn pensive and physically bothered, Kalen thought he would lighten the moment.

"Tough workout. Need to be prepared for Ethos Armageddon. Plus, it's part of concussion recovery. All about rhythm, flow, and focus." Not wanting to say more, Zane nodded and chuckled.

For a few seconds, Kalen appraised his best pal's demeanor and continued. "The calls for action are intensifying especially since the mural and campus riot. We've not arrived at consensus about what to support. Some propose further peaceful demonstration, while others are shouting for a *TIA* takedown. Although the 'how' of taking down the biotech firm is either nebulous or ridiculous depending on the post."

"Let's look at what's been achieved — either by us or by outcries that began right after the Earth event." Cali began to pace. "We wanted to build enough distrust and anger to create overwhelming social agreement to shut Ethos down. Honestly, I believe we're there. Other nations see what's happening here in the Southwest, and they've joined the sentiment to pause Ethos. International committees, boards, academics, even corporations have become quite vocal despite former alliances with *TIA*."

Zia got up from the floor cushion on which she was lounging. She strode over to the cool concrete surface of the wall. Placing both hands on the wall, she leaned in at a forty-degree angle for a full leg stretch.

Then, turning toward the group, Zia garnered attention. "The world may be against Ethos, but the kicker … is *TIA* listening? Willing to alter, pause, or put an end to the EthosBot? Has enough social pressure been exerted? As I see it, our next step is to push the biotech firm over the edge. Be the final pebble that tips the scale spurring the company to action … acknowledging their BioBot is devious. Devious enough to end." With that, she took up a yoga pose.

"Brilliant," Cali declared, resuming her restless pacing.

"If social resistance and call for action is not yet enough, then we need to ask ourselves what is their pain point? At the press release, they didn't admit Ethos was instrumental in the geomagnetic storm. They merely stated it was an experimental Crystal BioBot. Furthermore, they never explained how crystal energy combined with solar and electromagnetic forces to create the EcoSphere blowout. Although bound by employee confidentiality, my mother implies the EthosBot was a causative agent in the mayhem. At least, she hints as much. So, they're publicly denying or hiding."

Cali stopped pacing and whispered to her fellow schemers. "That's why mom is worn. More than I've ever seen. It's not just the beating she took during the riot. She's fighting with work. Her and Maya, her Co-Team Lead, are both in the thick of it with the corporate execs." The unexpected insight prompted Cali to put her hand to her mouth. She stared at Kalen.

"Likely, you're right. Mom heard you and Uncle Jake loud and clear the other night. I think it forced her to admit what she feels deep inside about Ethos but can't reconcile with the work she loves." Kalen absently rubbed his light beard.

Two of the windows were open bringing in fresh desert scent. Daylight was just beginning to fade. Autumn was pushing toward winter solstice with shorter days. Somewhere a pinyon fire smoldered. Cali and Zia particularly adored the fragrance, and breathing deeply, they both turned toward one another.

Centering, Cal. The scent takes us to a place of inner balance like nothing else does. Zia thought transferred to her best friend.

Cali relaxed letting her arms fall to her side. She closed

her eyes for mere seconds as she took in the scent of wood smoke.

The group remained quiet until a knock was heard on the door of their university business start-up — or more aptly put, the Project Crazy Paint hideaway in the university's concrete fortress.

Being the college student in charge, Nate strode to the door, opening it cautiously. The chalkboard was full of notes.

"Carson, hey, surprised to have you show up on a weekday for our get-togethers," Nate laughed. He opened the door wider.

The schemers welcomed their final teammate. Carson greeted Cali, placing his hands on her hips and giving her a gentle kiss on her cheek. "Hey, babe," he breathed, smelling clean and fresh but still like leather and earth.

Cali thought he appeared particularly pressed and dressed. *What's up?* She telepathed him.

"I'm taking you to dinner in town." He smiled at Cali, and then, not wanting to leave the group out, added a general invitation. "Hey, everyone can come really. I thought a night out would be fun with my girl, but we all need a break from Ethos doom."

Kalen watched as Carson towered physically over Cali. He was broad-shouldered, strong, and confident around her. Carson wasn't overbearing, but there were times when it was clear, he couldn't take his attention off Cal. It was cool, but as a brother, he felt protective.

Light conversation ensued, but no one was committing to a night on the town. There was even an exclamation from Nate or Zane, "You came for Cali, so take her out, bud."

Z spoke up. "Guys, schemers! Let's finish the pain point discussion thing. We need direction until we meet again."

In agreement to get back to business, the chatting and poking at one another quieted.

Cali cleared her throat and picked up her characteristic pace again. "Pain point, inflicting pain on *TIA*. We need the experts who can deride Ethos. Maybe not just those involved in the trials, but those who know enough to ridicule the science, and those who have enough respect to influence the corporate powers-that-be."

She snapped her fingers. "Where are we with trial volunteers? Do we have enough stories now to create a media clip or a scathing report?"

Now restless too, Kalen stood and closed one of the windows. Zia had shivered with the last gust. He began speaking as he locked the window.

"We've got over seventy or eighty reports from people who claim to have been patient volunteers in the trials. But here's the thing. We don't know if each is legit. Some who responded to our query about real-life experiences with Ethos testing could be activists seeking to fabricate stories just to feed social unrest and distrust. Volunteer patients need to be willing to authenticate their participation, so we can develop the game-changing report."

"What would verify their Ethos experience?" Zia spoke up. "They likely signed a lot of documents. Do you think they received patient copies? Or, as we've always wondered, does any trial participant still have the embedded BioBot? And, if there are some who still retain the devious bot, is it detectable? Could we verify the subcutaneous, that is, the subcu little bugger?"

Laughter churned. Z's comical nature made the most serious less so.

Smirking, Zane freely poked at his sister. "A certificate of completion like school. Oh no, wait. We'll use that old wand mechanism from the original health screening days when they looked for fluorescence. We'll just wave the wand over their arm and detect the bot."

At his friend's flippant remark, Kalen kicked at Zane's foot, then turned to Cali. "Cal, has Mom ever spoken or hinted about any who retained the EthosBot if it helped their anxiety or depression? Did she ever mention anything regarding the process of medical reporting?"

Cali shook her head in a negative reply as she pondered.

Then, Carson piped in. "There must be medical reports, and there are laws about patient access — regardless of clinical trial or approved for use medication, therapeutic, whatever ... We should assume the documentation is there. We just need one trial volunteer to share their info, and then we'll know what to ask for from others."

"And you know this how?" Cali was amazed at Carson's knowledge. "Are you an undercover agent pretending to be a rancher? Your business acumen is so noted at the hacienda, but healthcare and legal?"

Carson smirked. "University. Just like Nate. Plus, I had to navigate *T-Care* for my parents. Learned a thing or two about confidentiality, rights, and medical e-trails."

"The Ethos subcu presence," Nate sat up straight, shaking his hand at an important idea. "The old fluorescent wand deal to detect the original turamali virus is not too far off here. It's a crystal, guys. We can detect the presence of it. I mean the tool is used in physics and bioengineering all the time to detect force fields, even nanoscopic ones. It's not specific for Ethos, but what else would someone have subcu in that specific location? Demographic and access chips are different. We could identify Ethos with a small portable device."

"Wow, this just might be worthwhile then ... pursuing

as many of the cases as we can." Kalen considered further. "We don't want this becoming a months-long project, but we'll want enough clinical trial cases to come forward, so we have enough documentation for credibility. And, enough to cause alarm."

"Kalen, I'll do it with you," Zia offered. "We can schedule two at a time, and if we have short well-prepared questions, maybe we can get enough details in what? Thirty-minute interviews? Begin with virtual contact, securing document verification of participation. Or, if they are still wearing the bot, we rendezvous in person and use the device Nate describes. All anonymous but verifiable. We'll assign code names."

"I can help too," Cali blurted. "But first, I want to identify experts who weighed in on the science and development of Ethos, or better yet, conducted trials or evaluated the clinical outcomes. In media stories, most of the experts were quoted on behalf of *TIA*. Getting to the experts now in the middle of a social firestorm may be difficult. They're not likely to speak to a teenager on the hunt to take Ethos down. Honestly, since the Earth event, they're probably all in hiding."

Carson and Kalen dropped onto floor cushions. Cali and Zia still fidgeted and paced.

"Z," Zane interjected. "You know how to use the new software to setup case profiles? You'll need to set the searchable variables in advance — the ones you'll want to look at to create statistics. For instance, known demographics associated with certain mental health conditions ... age, gender, career, hallmark symptoms, telepathy status ... If you set that up in advance, the data automatically drops into place when you request that predictor model."

Zia shook her head affirmatively. "I can bring Kalen

and Cali up to speed quickly too. Plus, Kalen already has a handle on variables we should explore … from research and things his mother shared. He's also got insight from working with Kehlani and her telepathy classes. Kehl's got classes specifically for those who experience emotional suffering or difficulty."

"Z, you hit on something else." Kalen was excited. "Aunt Kehlani. She referred some from our telepathy classes to the EthosBot clinical trials at *TIA*. Maybe there's a way to get to those people. They might provide a different perspective … particularly if they witnessed the positive and negative outcomes with other volunteers."

"They'd be more likely to converse with us on the issue." Zia confirmed. "They know you and Kehlani. They might appreciate being heard. I admit, too, the devious bots likely did some good for some people, and our report should be balanced, fair." She breathed out and twisted her lips as if she didn't want to concede the bot had any merit.

"What? Did I hear you correctly, Z? A schemer softening on the devious little bot notion?" Zane teased his sister.

Giddy laughter followed for several minutes. The discussion was getting long and the day too.

Soon, with everyone conversing in the hallway about evening plans, Nate locked the schemers' hideaway door and faced the group.

Standing behind Cali, Carson's arms were wrapped around her waist while gently rocking and snuggling her neck. "Come on, schemers, let's hit the town. Light dinner, a few drinks — that is, whatever we can legally do based on age." He cajoled until the crew was convinced.

Chapter 7

GAME ON

Nestled among red rock buttes and high desert flora, the winding road dropped into an alternate universe for the tryst & schemers. Windows down, the fresh wind cleared troubled minds. The scent of chiminea fires permeated the air. Although each was different in character and demeanor, they shared the love of the Southwest and every bit of its sight, sound, scent, and vibe. You couldn't beat this town for exactly that.

The town retained historic roots with a few buildings dating back to the gold rush days. Newer structures were built with adobe in Pueblo or Territorial Revival styles. With *TuramaliScape* sitting several miles away, local citizens were determined to keep the essence and mixed cultures of the Southwest alive. Providing a unique escapism, the town flourished.

The trek into the humble Southwestern town was a thirty-minute jaunt in Carson's jeep. He offered to run everyone in, and then return everyone back to campus or home. Carson pulled up to their favorite haunt. Of course, it was Mexican food at its finest with comfortable ambiance.

Even though Carson's original intent had been an evening interlude with Cali, he accurately assumed all the schemers would cherish an escape from bot plotting. Thus, Carson had wisely reserved a larger outdoor table adjacent to one of the kiva-style fireplaces.

They found their places around a sturdy equipale table with cushioned benches and ordered ample libation and sustenance. Between the drive into the crisp night air and feeding physical hunger, the schemers fell into conversation about their next outing on horseback.

Midway through plotting their next adventure, Cali's attention suddenly landed on a new group taking a table in another corner of the outdoor patio. Gabe caught her eye at the same time. He smiled broadly and without hesitation, walked over to Cali.

Coming up smoothly behind and placing both hands on her shoulders, he greeted the companions. "Hola, Cali, how are you? Hey, all!"

Flabbergasted by the unexpected move by Gabe, Cali blushed and tried to recover without her friends noticing. As if they were old acquaintances, she quickly put one of her hands on Gabe's as it rested on her shoulder, rolling her lower lip inward as she pulled off a contorted smile.

"Everyone, this is Gabe. He's the medic who saved my mom and me from the campus riot and stayed with us until we got to *T-Care*."

Carson was unnerved, but worse, he was unsure why. "Thanks for saving my girl," he responded. "The medics are out for a night of fun too?"

"This place has become our routine getaway, but only when we can manage time together. Gotta love the salsa and margaritas. Well, I won't keep you. Nice meeting everyone."

Gabe gave Cali's shoulders a final squeeze and dragged

his one hand purposefully beneath her hair and across her neck. Cali felt the touch deep inside.

What the heck is happening? Cali kept the wonder to herself.

Carson did what any guy would do when he felt threatened by a competitor. He pushed Cali's hair aside and kissed her cheek. Then he jostled his seat and leg closer to her. He sensed tension, but decided it was unfounded. He thought, this Gabe is flirting, and she's responding like any teen. I refuse to be that jealous guy.

Seated across from Cali, Zia waited for the right moment. When Carson was looking away, Zia stared at Cali, tilting her head and raising her eyebrows. *What up, Cali Cal?*

Zia didn't anticipate a response, but she recognized it in her best friend's face. *We've got trouble in Turamali City. That's T that rhymes with B and stands for boyfriend. Boyfriend trouble.*

Cali got the thought transmission. Clear and hit to the core, as only a trusted friend could do to another with respectful intent.

Kalen caught the exchange, the cautious looks and overtone, but did not want to engage. Pulled from the Gabe affair, he began picking up on comments from a nearby table with at least a dozen people tightly circled around two tables. Low conversation progressively escalated such that Kalen captured certain words that aroused suspicion.

"Guys, I think we hit turamali gold. Yo, all. Hear me." When Kalen had his compadres' attention, he adamantly whispered. "That table over there ... I think they're Ethos clinical trial ... talking about experiences. A couple are rubbing their arms like maybe where the BioBot was placed. I think we should approach them. Our case studies just may have fallen into our laps."

Discreetly and together, Cali and Zia attempted to intercept any telepathic messaging they could from the intimately hunched-together group just feet away.

Simultaneously, Cali and Zia nodded and affirmed, "Yeah." "Yup."

"Who goes over there, and how do we engage without alarm?" Cali asked looking around the table. They were nearly done with their meals, and it was getting time to head home.

It was quickly agreed that Zia and Kalen should approach the group, as they were now delegated the task of garnering Ethos trial stories. After a brief huddle, the schemers had a plan.

Zia took the lead as she and Kalen drew adjacent to the group. "Hi, we apologize for interrupting, but we believe we share something in common." Sitting taller in their seats with serious expressions, they turned their attention to Zia. One pair, a man and a woman, waved a hand indicating to proceed.

"I'm Zia. This is Kalen. We're developing an exposé about EthosBot. It's ... it's part of a university project we're working on. I mean, we're doing it independently. We're trying to get to the truth about this BioBot. Is it healing emotional and mental states of unease, or is it creating havoc such as the recent geomagnetic storm?"

Observing skepticism and agitation among the circle of huddled friends, Zia paused. Then Kalen jumped in.

"I thought I heard references to the Ethos clinical trials. I didn't mean to eavesdrop. Honestly, please, we want to develop a report about the experiences of volunteers we can verify."

Feeling encouraged, Z picked up the thread. "Since

the Earth event, the media is riddled with comments and stories about the effects of EthosBot, but how many posts are true versus geared to inciting fear? If you were indeed clinical volunteers, you'd be sharing your experience with others, and we're trusting your stories would be enough to prompt an end to Ethos if that's what's best."

"Anonymous," Kalen tagged. "Anyone who shares, we'll make sure there is no way to trace the personal experience back to you."

As Zia and Kalen spoke, shoulders relaxed, hands fiddled with drinks, but uneasy glances still abounded.

The wiry gentleman who initially encouraged their interaction queried. "Your friends — they're a part of this exposé as you refer to it? You see, if we are who you believe we are, we need to limit risk. We need to know more."

"Agree," Kalen was quick to respond. "This isn't the time or place either. I'll leave our contact info, both mine and Zia's. If you want to alter the trajectory of Ethos, reach out to us ... soon, very soon. We'll set up a private site to meet, and we can cover details. A place to speak freely." Kalen had already written their contact details on a paper napkin, and he eagerly gave it to the de facto spokesperson of the group.

"A site on campus? You mentioned university. We ... we need to feel we'd be going to a safe location."

Uncertain, Zia and Kalen both sighed. Nate could probably secure additional university space. Or they could use their current entrepreneurial hub — although revealing the hideaway to anyone outside their inner circle carried risk of exposure.

Cali quietly walked up next to Zia. "I'm Cali. Sage Amaris' daughter. We're asking for your help. We simply want the truth about Ethos. Please."

Expressions showed stun and astonishment. Fidgeting stopped. The quiet of the group was deafening. Even the noisy chatter of other tables faded without perception.

Cali's courageous and risky introduction ended the dialogue. Sage Amaris' daughter. Sage of original eco-bot fame.

Zane, Nate, Carson, and Kalen headed toward the patio gate to depart. Three from the accosted group rose and made their way to Cali. They each gave her a hug and a whisper.

Game on.

Cali was the last to slide into Carson's jeep. Rather than snugged against her beau, she squished next to Kalen and Zia. In a trance, she slumped, leaning against the open window as it blew her hair in all directions. Perhaps, more than one game … on.

Chapter 8

COERCION

Sabino was following Cali to the gate and trailhead, as Kalen led Kona by a lead rope loosely circled around the gelding's neck. Except for a thick saddle pad, the teens were headed out bareback. Early Saturday morning brought light cool breezes and a gorgeous cerulean sky — an idyllic day for a ride to incite forgetfulness and find that place where inner spirit soars. Sabino and Kona were perfect companions for such an endeavor.

"Cali, Kalen," their father shouted. They turned and spied Uncle Cyprus.

Cali messaged Kalen. *So early in the morning. What's Uncle Cy doing here? He's semi-official agent looking too. Pressed khakis and a dark polo.*

Bayani strode toward the twins. "Let Kona and Sabino go. You're going with Uncle Cy to his headquarters."

Not believing their father was serious, the twins hesitated. *Cal, we've been had.* Kalen messaged his sister.

In daughter-like-mother fashion, Cali wanted to hop on Sabino and gallop away. Ride and run until the world was behind her. She wasn't sure what was weighing more heavily on her — her affair of the heart or Ethos drama. *I'm too young for this. So are you, Kalen. Let's blow this taco stand.*

I would, Cal, for anyone other than Uncle Cy. He's got a job to do, but he's on our side. We ... we can't run. Not now.

With that telepathic message, spontaneous enlightenment ran through Kalen from head to toe and seemingly through the very ground on which he stood. The sensation nearly paralyzed him. *Not running yet anyway.* Was the unsettling message from his own consciousness or from where? Weirder, the phrase implied there would soon be a time to run.

Cyprus detected Cali's hesitancy, and *sensing* what he'd come to know as her need to run, he telepathed directly to her. *Cali, it's me ... beneath the demeanor of an agent.* He strode toward her and standing a few feet from her and Sabino, he patiently waited for her choice.

Cali placed her hands on Sabino's neck. "Later." Acknowledging the release, Sabino nudged Cali's shoulder. The mare's nostrils flared slightly with the breath of sweet grass hay. Together, Sabino and Kona meandered toward Bayani. The saddle pads at least needed to be taken off and hung.

Bayani and Sage watched as their teens were whisked to FSPA headquarters nearby. Meanwhile, Cali and Kalen were quiet in the Float3 as it jettisoned off into the desert to a remote location.

♦

Kalen and Cali were escorted by Uncle Cy and another agent to a conference room that thankfully had windows and comfortable chairs. Unfortunately, Cyprus hit an icon on a nearby panel, and shades rumbled halfway down blocking the serenity of the desert. Surely the meaning of this cozy chat was becoming obvious.

"I need you to sit together on one side of the table."

The teens looked at one another, and Cali moved to sit next to her brother. The other agent stood near the door, arms casually at his side. Something about him, though, screamed readiness.

Uncle Cy stood in front of the table facing the teens he knew so well. His arms were crossed in front of his chest. Affixed to a lanyard, his agent badge was pushed up awkwardly by his arms, but it didn't appear to bother Uncle Cy. As if acknowledging the atypical workday, his man bun hung loosely but dark hair strands were tidy. His swarthy complexion showed signs of occupational wear, but the Radiance BioBot had instilled the familiar healthy glow. Federal agent, Cyprus Desai carried the ever-present sense of calm which emanated beyond what most people could muster.

"Cali, Kalen, thank you for coming freely today. As you realize, your birth parents agreed to this informal inquiry. Otherwise, we may have been forced to take an aggressive approach — which of course, we wanted to avoid. I need to ask you some questions about recent activities. You won't be recorded, but I will write up a few notes about our conversation. Any questions?"

Cyprus walked the line between intimidating the teens he loved and gently persuading. He had to establish the seriousness of the business at hand, but neither did he want to frighten them into holding their secrets.

Cy pondered for a moment. He didn't want to rush. I see Sage sitting before me. Nearly twenty years ago. The reincarnated Rebel times two.

Now, placing both hands firmly on the table in front of Cali and Kalen, he leaned forward looking intently at the teens' upturned faces. "Tell me about Project Paint or Crazy Paint."

Brother and sister tilted their heads at one another, both afraid to telepath a word.

Kalen tried to appear calm. Using a few seconds to gather thoughts, he tapped his fingers on the table. "Where did you hear the term Project Paint? Was it one of us or one of our friends?" Kalen almost used the descriptor 'schemers' instead of friends. They may call themselves tryst & schemers, but the outside world had to see them with less mischief.

"Where we heard it does not concern you. Project Paint. What does it mean to you?"

"It's a silly project name we gave to rehabilitating Zane's American Paint horse, Desperado. After the crazy mare unseated Zaner, we thought we could do more to help Desperado be less spooky. Natural horsemanship techniques." Cali's voice was reserved as she attempted to give a plausible story.

"Kalen, is that right?" Since Cy had a close relationship with Kalen, he felt compelled to push for the truth.

Kalen merely nodded.

"Nothing related to the painting, the 'End Ethos' mural on a concrete wall of *TuramaliScape?*"

Now, both teens sat straighter and protested. "No, no, Project Paint has nothing to do with that."

"Bad timing," Kalen explained further. "We came up with the name after river tubing … the night you all went to Aunt Kehlani's and Uncle Jake's, while we had a firepit cookout with the ranchers."

Cyprus smiled. "Ah. Then how's Desperado's training

coming along? She more tolerant of spooky situations? … How often are you and your pals working with her? Is Carson helping? Bayani? He's a Spanish horse whisperer."

The teens squirmed. Caught. Once, Kalen worked with Zane taking Desperado through various challenges — such as wind-tossed paper bags, sudden blanket shaking to the side of her vision, noisy machinery, and typical actions or situations that could startle. Desperado was high strung but already steady when faced with challenges. The Earth event had simply been too much for the energetic Paint horse. The one meager training session before Ethos mania wouldn't be enough to counter Uncle Cy's implication.

An excruciatingly long minute passed. Then another.

Jeez, Uncle Cy, you're good at this. In frustration, Kalen telepathed hoping to lighten the questioning.

In response to Kalen's message, Cy gave a light laugh. "We noticed you purchased chalk. Was the mural supposed to be done in chalk?"

"What's happening here, Uncle Cy?" Cali's eyes filled with tears. She was mad and hurt. "Are you tracking our purchases? Our conversations? Is it legal to wiretap us or sneak into our telepathic transmissions? Surveil what teens are saying, doing? … We're your spiritual, adopted daughter and son, extended family thing … uniquely conjured by our famous parents …" The rambling stopped.

The other agent placed a tissue box on the table in front of Cali. She shook her head and knitted her eyebrows. *This is so not right.* In protest, she wiped tears with her shirt sleeve and pushed the tissue box away.

Cyprus didn't want to carry on the investigation too long. Neither did he want to distress the teens beyond any trust in him. He would need their faith and conviction when all was said and done. The goal was not to break their unusually strong characters.

With a final push, he queried, "How about DustDevil, TripleTempest? That mean anything to you?" Cy rubbed his chin and paced. "Guys. Cal, Kalen. Hear me. Just tell me the truth. It doesn't need to go beyond these walls. I need to know … hear it from you."

Another minute of silence. This time, controlled by the teens.

They were furious. How were their actions revealed?

Kalen pivoted in the swivel chair to face Cali. She followed with the same motion. Deeply looking into each other's eyes for mere seconds, they discovered what they should do at this moment in time. It wasn't a haunting or probing stare. It was mere soul communication between twins born in the Age of Turamali.

"We'll tell you, Uncle Cy. Most of it anyway. Minus the minutiae. Deal?" Cali rallied.

Kalen clarified. "Uncle Cy, as part of the deal, you leave us alone. We're moving ahead on … on our intentions, our plans."

"My dear Cali and Kalen, I will try my best to leave you to your wiles … as long as no one is the target of harm, either directly or indirectly. What I can promise you is that before you leave today, we will have a clear understanding of expectations … what I won't interfere in, but perhaps what I need you to back down on."

"We don't have a choice really." Cali whispered, then sighed. A rogue tear ran down her cheek. Barely audible, she added, "We need to finish our work on Ethos. There's too much at stake to not follow through on our scheme."

"The schemers will be allowed to go on." Cy winked at them. He wanted to squeeze their hands in encouragement, but he needed to finish this foray professionally.

"I'm listening."

Cy gave the stand-by-the-door agent a cue. The agent retrieved mineral-infused waters and placed them in front of the teens. Perhaps Uncle Cy believed the discussion would be long and thirst-provoking.

Uneasy about how much time this would take and how much would eventually be revealed, Kalen drank and then twirled the water glass. Elbows on the table, he looked at Cali and nodded for her to begin.

"The mission of Project Paint is to discredit the EthosBot. We're building on the fear and mistrust that was sown by the Earth event. Just adding fuel to the fire that's already mainstream. TripleTempest and DustDevil are our cyber aliases. We participate in social media conversations, and we also create our own dialogue.

"We've spent quite a bit of time perusing the company's publications and announcements especially as related to the clinical trials. The purpose is to figure out what happened in the trials. What were the clinical outcomes? Were people better? Did some retain the subcu BioBot?

"To bring home the reality of Ethos, we intend to post an exposé based on trial volunteer experiences. We've just started that process, and it will be unbiased. We'll report the positive and negative."

Cali took a drink and looked away. She telepathed her brother. *I don't want to mention the expert I identified. Not worth it. Don't want to risk his exposure and doesn't add anything to what Uncle Cy needs to know.*

In response, he jostled his knee against hers. *Agree.*

"The mural, the chalk?" Cyprus probed.

Kalen stated firmly, "We had nothing to do with the mural or the activists that day. Like everyone else, we read the snippets of conversation implying action, but all that took us by surprise too. The chalk ... well the chalk ..." Recalling how difficult it was to locate old-fashion chalk, he chuckled.

"The chalk was an interesting task to find and purchase. Uncle Cy, we needed the chalk to use an old schoolhouse chalkboard we found at an antique market." Kalen sighed heavily. These funny meaningless details seemed a joke now. "We use the chalkboard to plot and plan. It's a list of tasks. Honestly, we like the easy utility of it, and our work can't be traced. We simply erase. Erase the chalk, every implicating note."

Kalen was proud of their chalkboard idea. He chuckled again and gave Uncle Cy a smirk.

Rubbing his chin, Cy paced. "Who are the Triple-Tempest and DustDevil? It appears the moniker 'tryst & schemers' includes a group. Cal, Kalen, who is involved with you?"

On this query, the twins hesitated.

Kalen shook his head in a negative manner. *Can't throw our fellow schemers under the bus.*

"Was it your pal, Nate, who put together a way to reroute your electronic communications? We're familiar with his particular skill set. I'll tell you this much ... We can read your posts just like the rest of the world can. Something in those conversations told us the author had to be the offspring of someone working at *TIA*. Or how else would someone know? We also know how angry and determined the two of you have been since the Earth event."

More silence.

"Kalen, Cali, who? Who's involved in this with you two? Where do you meet?"

Rising from the chair, Kalen stood up tall and stared at his Uncle Cy. He tapped his fingers nervously on the table.

He could feel a tirade coming on.

"Federal Agent Cyprus Desai … we … we are not divulging who are fellow schemers are, nor our location."

Joining her brother in solidarity, Cali stood. She pushed back her shoulders with arms tense at her side. "We'll call Aunt Jen if you push us any further. No matter what our parents agreed to, we'll take legal representation."

The guardian-of-the-door agent shifted forward. He rested his hand on his belt and weapon.

Cy waved the agent-in-arms back. Studying the teens he'd help rear, he tightened his lips, breathed in deeply, and puffed out his chest.

"If Project Paint is a media campaign to undermine the EthosBot, I don't need anything further. If there is no discussion or intent to destroy property, break and enter, or conduct any illegal act, we're done here.

"I am curious about the sophisticated masking or firewall one of your compatriots has hobbled together." Cy looked for any visual sign one of them would be willing to offer up this piece of information. Seeing no acquiescence, he stated, "For a future discussion."

"We don't expect to be followed or surveilled. We've established there are no grounds for suspecting illegal activity. Correct?" Cali sought confirmation the tryst & schemers need not be paranoid, nor looking over their shoulders.

"Cali Rose Amaris Casander and Sami Kalen Amaris Casander, we're done here. Unless I have reason to believe you are in danger, you will not be under surveillance. Keep the social media dialogue above reproach. And as a favor … when the exposé of the trial volunteers is composed, would you send it prior to posting? Only if you're willing. Anything to help the FSPA prepare for potential fallout from the report."

In deference, Cali and Kalen shrugged. "Yeah, sure."

Cy tapped the table. "Remember, that chalkboard only hides your secrets if you erase it before it's seen by those seeking to monitor or disrupt your efforts." He winked at his teens. "Let's get outta here and enjoy a Saturday."

The twins stood waiting beside the Float3 for Uncle Cy to take them home to the ranch. He finished conversing with his colleague at the building entrance and unlocked the vehicle as he strode toward them. He tossed his badge on the open console. Since access for nearly everything was via embedded chip, the badge was a nuisance, an appendage, a visual leftover from bygone days. However, the visual made a statement, and now it told the teens their Uncle Cy was done for the day. He was now their Uncle Cyprus.

Cali and Kalen had been deep in conversation, and although they were anxious to depart, they still stood adjacent to the operator's side of the vehicle where Cyprus would take his seat. Cy looked at his kids. After all, he was an integral part of the multi-parenting commitment made at their birth.

The soft interrogation left him feeling somber. He sincerely believed Cali and Kalen were behind the thematic painting of the *T-Scape* wall and had fallen in with social activists. Evidently not. However, he had a job to do, and for mental sanity, he needed to know if his kids — Sage's, Bayani's, Jake's, Kehlani's, and Jen's too — were safe and uncoerced into anything related to violence or unlawful action. He'd been conflicted. By ethical standards, he should have excused himself from the task, but instead, he had insisted on personally conducting an off-the-books dialogue with the teens.

Uncle Cy pulled Cali into a rocking bear hug. His one hand caressed the back of her head, and then he kissed her forehead. Then, he gave a manly hug with a gentle slap on the back to Kalen.

"You owe us, Uncle Cy. For not believing in us. Dragging us down here." Kalen wanted to say more, but when he saw the look on his uncle's face, he knew he'd hit home. Enough. Plus, the hug had softened Kalen's frustration.

"Perhaps, I do," Cyprus said quietly, not sure what to make of the teens' body language. There was something more on their minds.

Cali smirked. "We've got plans for you. The rest of Saturday we're supposed to enjoy? You're doing it with us. You're coming on a trail ride. That bonding thing that parents talk and care about especially as their kids get older? Well, time you rode our trail with us ... see our world."

Cyprus laughed heartily. "You know, I'm just a lump of a trail rider. I can't keep up with you two."

"You and Aunt Jen have come a long way over the years. I know you don't ride much. But, we're taking you out. Now." Cali was adamant. "Your clothes and shoes should work. We'll put you on my dad's horse, Dakota, with a saddle." She tilted her head sideways in a mischievous manner. "We decided not to send you out bareback with no bridle."

All three laughed. The weight and worry, the veil of suspicion lifted.

As promised, Cali and Kalen made Uncle Cyprus pay. They returned to the ranch, and with Bayani and Carson's assistance, the horses were readied.

Setting an easy but bright pace, Cali led the ride on Sabino. Uncle Cy followed on Dakota with Kalen bringing up the rear astride Kona. Where the trail widened, the teens moved to either side of Uncle Cy. This was a family outing, and they were determined to talk up a storm with their uncle. It was time he was part of their conversation — from school and relationships to river tubing and next adventures, from bots and biotech to saving the world. They argued, challenged, laughed, and at times, enjoyed private thought.

It was Agent Desai, Uncle Cy's turn to be coerced. Coerced by Cali and Kalen and the open space of the Southwest.

Chapter 9

FAILED ATTEMPTS

Doctor Rane welcomed Cali into his home. "Sage's daughter," he greeted her with unexpected admiration and respect. He firmly took Cali's hand in his, embracing it like a favorite crystal and looking deeply into her eyes. "Yes. You most certainly are her offspring. I can see the spirit. The 'I won't back down'. You're smart like her too. My dear, your brilliance is coming."

Not anticipating warm familiarity and essentially a reading of her nature, Cali blushed and faltered. "My mother ... sends her greeting. She wishes you could help the teams now with EthosBot."

"My dear Cali. Don't feel timid. I'm just an old codger. Come, let's head to my study and chat."

Dr. Rane's home was located just outside the nearby historic town. It was a new development of adobe-themed architecture with modern adjustments to enhance natural light and accommodate sophisticated technologies. The study or home library, however, was a throwback. Natural mango wood shelves spanned floor to ceiling with books. There was not simply one desk but three, and they were all covered in more books and stacks of paper. Pottery of the Southwest, fashioned stone figurines, colorful kachinas carved from cottonwood, and storyteller clay sculptures were positioned strategically amid paper chaos.

The endless shelves of books drew her in first. Upon seeing the multitude of printed works, Cali exclaimed, "Wow. You don't just possess a few tomes. You've got bound books everywhere."

Having only read about the concept of former libraries with endless rows and floors of printed works, Cali was entranced. Aunt Jen and her mom had modest bookcases, but this display was remarkable. "Is this what a library used to look like?"

Crouching and then up on tip toe, she moved slowly across the shelves to view and touch. "Dr. Rane, these are beautiful. Are the ones with embossed gold lettering more important? People really spent money on books and kept them even after reading?"

She turned to see Dr. Rane sitting in a plush leather chair adjacent to the room's decorative kiva fireplace.

He chuckled, "Ah, youth. We did spend quite a bit on books, and the ones we enjoyed or treasured, we kept. Some of the medical references in psychiatry and parapsychology, I used my entire career. My parents were both professors, and I grew up in university libraries. So, although books have a place in my medical profession, they also hold nostalgia, charm, and comfort. As you've noted, some are simply beautiful to behold."

Cali gently touched a sculpted stone figurine adorned with turquoise and coral. "So beautiful," she whispered. "Dr. Rane, are the pottery and carvings all Native American?"

She moved from one desk to another, gently touching

each artistic piece as if she needed to feel the magic. Wondering if she could handle some, Cali glanced at Dr. Rane who knowingly nodded affirmatively. On a few pots of various shapes, she ran her fingers over the etchings taking in the intricate designs and colors.

"Enchanting, captivating ..." Cali was spellbound by the artisan works.

"Mostly, I collected Navajo, Zuni, and Hopi. Each has a story." He sighed heavily. "I used to remember every artist, every roadside stand and pueblo where I found each treasure. Cali, my memory fades too much these days ... Come sit with me. Let's talk BioBots."

Cali sank into the comfort of a plush chair opposite Dr. Rane. The leather was soft, and the high back and ample armrests soothed her earlier nervousness.

"You know, I was with your mother in the thick of the original eco-bot drama. I was drawn in with the Biologics & Intelligent Life Team to help solve the mystery of how a turamali-driven bot with an engineered virus to save botanical life could end up giving humans telepathy. And not only telepathy, but hallucination, impaired cognition, hyperintelligence ... Well, I'm sure your mother told you the story."

"Dr. Rane, you were the hero. You discovered the link between the botanical virus and heightened susceptibility of a specific human neurotransmitter ... which happened as people simply ingested crops, botanical life. I remember the story about those who gained telepathy early on from eating prickly pear jam!" Composed and comfortable now, Cali prattled on, as Dr. Rane smiled and nodded entertained and flattered.

"You were the one to explain how turamali inadvertently affected normal psychoactive receptors. Interestingly, it was the same psychoactive receptor triggered by magic mushrooms and psychedelic drugs. You solved the riddle, and then you helped orchestrate the entire public health screening program ... which gained notoriety for identifying health trends and the natural spread of the phenomenon. The methods and statistical models you developed are still being used. You were even part of the famous *Mission: Turamali* in Asia."

"You've done your homework, or at least your mother spun a decent tale about who I am and what I've done. She was a joy to work with. Quite the feisty personality too. But it was who she was and is ... fearless and either reckless or brave in her action to launch the bots that forever changed Earth. I do miss her, Cali. Too, I miss the excitement and challenge of being a part of something so momentous." He looked wistful.

Cali waited a moment for the nostalgic memories to settle. Gently, she probed for the information she desired. "Dr. Rane, we're developing an exposé about what happened during clinical trials ... beyond the published outcome data. We want your insight on the science and physiology behind Ethos and how the trials were carried out."

Without actively thought messaging, she wondered. I really want to know if Ethos works. Is it a legit efficacious BioBot?

"Right. The 'we' in all this — you mentioned your brother, Kalen, and then four other companions. I'll tell you what you need to know, and Cali ... I will be clear about what you can quote, and on what aspects I must remain anonymous. It's a dicey situation out there with Ethos. Everyone's stirred up one way or another. I have strict confidentiality agreements, but at my age, not sure even *TIA* would come after me. Better to err on the side of keeping things peaceful." He thrummed the armrests and watched as Cali opened an electronic tablet to record notes.

"First, you need to indulge me a bit as I describe the challenges of mental health. That backdrop is critical for understanding why Ethos has taken years to develop, and it's debatable whether we've achieved what we set out to do.

"The dance between biology and our emotional response to life events is mysterious. Being a medical psychiatrist, I can tell you we understand far less than we pretend to know. Worse, what we think we know, we have only fooled ourselves into believing we know.

"Mental and emotional health are as real as the health of the physical body, and truly, it is all physical. The physiology of our head-to-toe body is intricately linked to the feeling of wellbeing and vice versa. One creates the other. The broken heart and stomach butterflies are based in biology and feedback loops.

"It's quite fragile, my dear Cali. We've played at treating mental states with all types of therapies and enough prescription medication to choke a horse — as the saying goes. Some honestly helped, others not. Tolerable side effects and sometimes not. Messing with mental and emotional states impacts mood, personality, judgment, the very foundation of how someone views the world around them. My colleagues and I treaded on difficult unstable terrain for decades, centuries really."

Cali observed Dr. Rane as he expounded and philosophized. His hair was fully gray and nearly touching the collar of this shirt. No balding and surprisingly not too thin. His complexion revealed age but with a healthy blush. Surely, the series of Radiance BioBots over recent years elevated the vigorous professor and wizard appearance. Yet, fatigue and sadness appeared to run deep.

"Despite hurdles in treating mental states, the concept of the Ethos BioBot was worth pursuing? You supported it? Was it different for you than conventional treatment?"

"Some of us believed that crystal therapy would heal mental states the same way as the eco-bot transformed Earth, and the Radiance and Assault BioBots tackled common ailments and disease." He sighed heavily, as if the assumption was now questionable.

"The eco-bot restored ecosystems. The Radiance and Assault outright healed and cured. Would a Crystal BioBot for the mind relieve anxiety, cure depression, and bring on a steady, balanced, happy demeanor? Fix attention deficit or bipolar disorder? The list of conditions which plague our brains, our neurons ... is long.

"Thus, we focused on the two most common conditions, anxiety and depression. New Age spiritualism lent us a hand there. Several crystals are known to alleviate symptoms, such as amethyst, tourmaline, lapis, citrine, aquamarine, smoky and rose quartz. The major catch is the individual and how they respond to a specific crystal's vibrational energy. The science of crystal healing was foundationally different for mental ailments.

"For instance, hematite in the Assault Bot targets infection no matter individual characteristics and all due to its structure and specific mineral composition. The Assault plain and simple terminates pathogens. The Radiance goes right for the bones and joints ... again no matter the person. Once we elucidated the science, we found these crystals are naturally designed to miraculously heal.

"However, EthosBot crystals for mental disturbances uniquely depend on the individual. We were staring down customized, personalized medicine in a way that befuddled and challenged in a manner not encountered in the history of medicine. Don't get me wrong — we've achieved custom BioBots for cancers, but that is narrowly focused on a relatively common set of errant mutations. Plus, it's cell-based stuff we can elucidate, see, touch with lab tools.

"In contrast, how does one elucidate, see, manipulate the highly intricate biochemical communication occurring in each person's brain? How does one discover a person's ethos, figure out the wayward mechanism and fix it?

"Say for instance, we had fifty volunteers with diagnosed anxiety or combined anxiety and depression. With more than a dozen different crystals before them, responses were as variable as the fifty people. To complicate the whole darn mess, each type of crystal has a different atomic structure often evidenced by color. For instance, tourmaline is a family of minerals with an array of lovely colors. Rose quartz is not always simply rose quartz. It could be rose or pink which are considered different varieties. Imagine the common crystals we can freely name, then multiply that by varieties of each, then the presence of trace elements … Cali, how does one begin to match each person's affliction with such a universe of potential crystal properties?

"Too, the confounders were overwhelming. This just wasn't the same as treating an infection or degenerative back pain or arthritis. People's daily lives fluctuated with exposure to daily stresses — family, work, school, and social conditions. Amethyst may have helped an individual for a month or two, then suddenly became useless against their anxiety. Each person's triggers were as unique as the crystal they chose and all with variable clinical response time." Dr. Rane was becoming agitated at the memory of the complexity of EthosBot development.

"Cali, the trials were conducted soundly. The trial outcomes were not what we'd hoped for — at least from a scientific, statistical perspective. In one trial, thirty-three percent achieved successful crystal therapy. In another trial, fifty-eight percent. Then fifteen and eighty-two percent. What do you do with that kind of outcome data?

"We took a hard look at every aspect of the clinical trials." He shrugged. "We got good at creating lists of study limitations and more confounders. It was tedious and fatiguing."

"You'd helped some people though. The published reports indicate that many were grateful for the relief they did receive for whatever time they participated. A few were quoted as saying the clinical trial had taught them to work through their troubled mental state and forever improved their perspective on how to live with purpose and intention."

Responding to Dr. Rane's agitation, Cali tried to be upbeat. Too, she wanted a balanced report — the healed, not healed, frustration, side effects, and more.

"True, we had some volunteers who kept their customized Crystal BioBot subcutaneously for only a few months, and then appeared remarkably healed. With follow-up a year later, many remained anxiety or depression-free. But for every success, it seemed we had a failure."

"Dr. Rane, I have some difficult, pointed questions. Did patient cases keep the EthosBot implanted beneath their skin after completion of the trial? Are there people around us now with embedded EthosBots? Secondly, are the trials ongoing? Finally, would you say the EthosBot is a success or failure?"

He pushed himself away from the leather chair and smiled. "How do I answer you, Cali?" Being somewhat stiff, he ambled with purpose toward the paired patio doors. Upon opening, the scent of creosote was pungent. "The fragrance of a brief but fresh rain. It's marvelous."

Stepping toward the patio, she joined Dr. Rane in the conversational interlude about bots. "I adore the scent of the desert. It's better than a crystal sometimes. It fills every part of the soul, doesn't it? And all you need do is wander into the desert."

"Yes, I suppose it does fill the soul. It's why I've never moved despite tantalizing career options." He studied Cali. "Exposé. Figured we get to the hard stuff. Yes, there are trial volunteers among us who have the EthosBot embedded. It makes sense though, right? They came to *TIA* to participate, but they certainly went home after scheduled treatment or evaluation days. For those it helped, they kept their subcu bot. Over the years, probably treated several thousand. I can't say more on that.

"Are trials still being conducted? By my own choice, I'm no longer involved directly in the clinical trials. However, I would imagine they are ongoing. Something you may wheedle out of your mother.

"Success or failure? Is it my place to judge, Cali? I'll tell you this. By medical standards, interventions and medications need to meet criteria for effectiveness and safety. Basically, it begs the query: Did the intervention do what it was supposed to do, and do so without undue harm? For example, did the surgical procedure fix the injury and do so without causing worse problems? Furthermore, it is also against similar standards by which side effects and complications are deemed acceptable or not.

"Statistically, Ethos failed. It was not found significantly efficacious on any parameter. Clinically, it was successful for some, others not. Those who have improved or healed are living a life they thought not possible prior to the EthosBot. For those, Ethos is efficacious. But the overall numbers, those positively impacted have not been enough to make Ethos a realistic treatment option for anxiety or depression for the masses.

"By medical standards, is the EthosBot safe? Some employees conducting the clinical trials became disoriented, emotionally stressed. At first, we couldn't figure out what was happening. When they were removed from the premises, they reverted to wellbeing within a matter of days or weeks. Based on sickened employees and the Earth event, I'd say Ethos failed to meet criteria for safety. By my estimation, Ethos in its current form is reckless.

"For the world, is Ethos achieving what the Radiance and Assault series of BioBots have? Could it be a win for humanity and for those with whom we share the planet?" He paused and pushed gray strands of hair away from his cheek.

"Could it be reengineered to be safe and efficacious one day? It's for you and your generation to decide and judge the merits. Cali, my time on neurons and BioBots is at an end."

Until this point, Dr. Rane obviously enjoyed sharing what he knew, but now he appeared despondent. The ominous tone of finality perturbed Cali.

Dr. Rane breathed deeply. "What else? What didn't I cover?"

"Oh, the recent Earth event ... how was that related to the EthosBot? Or indeed has Ethos been falsely accused of the sandstorm and electromagnetic field disruption?"

"Hhhmmm ... we did encounter dangerous force fields along the way. Storing and working with such a wide array of crystals did have notable repercussions. When staff become emotionally disoriented, we called Hailey Emir the geophysicist for assistance. The EMF and seismography readings around *TuramaliScape* were astounding. She stated the field intensity exceeded what she discovered two decades ago when some of the original hovercraft failed. Back then, the hovercraft biomechanically fried in the field — supposedly when the crystal energy of the eco-bot met up with certain geographic EMFs. With Ethos, we had a couple of incidents of barely perceptible earthquakes which Hailey confirmed.

"Now, it seems the creation of Radiance and Assault BioBots in tandem with Ethos is clearly too much crystal vibrational energy in one geographic location." He chuckled. "We even called in one of the local Adepts, and she along with the geophysicist confirmed the shifting of ley lines on the planet. The Adept, Kehlani Rose, declared new ley lines are forming. You know Cali, those presumptive, spiritual energy fields around the pyramids, ancient ruins …" He waved an arm as if he doubted the reality of ley lines or at least where they resided.

"The whole mess not entirely understood. But I will tell you this. Once we began the trials, some workers were affected adversely, developing the very state of anxiety they were evaluating. What exactly occurred a few weeks ago — being called a solar EMF amplified storm — I don't know. I would not be surprised if it was related to Ethos. That bot has stirred up some kind of supernatural vibration — measurable, tangible to our senses, but elusive."

"Why did the trials move forward if *TIA* employees had such noticeable effects from being around the EthosBot?"

"My colleagues and I debated. Yet, we believed or wanted to believe that even if some could be helped by Ethos, it was worth the effort and risk. We simply excused staff and shuffled around some processes to decrease the overall exposure at *TIA* and *TuramaliScape* as a campus."

"Dr. Rane, was any BioBot development moved offsite?

Were trials moved to other locales?" Cali was not sure why this question popped into her head, but she pursued it. If changes were made to decrease exposure, didn't it imply that crystals and bots were relocated?

"Said you were smart. Intuitive too." Folding arms across his chest in a protective manner, Dr. Rane studied Cali's face. "On this aspect, don't push. I cannot say."

Cali allowed silence to fall between them. The double French patio doors shifted with an incoming breeze.

He walked to the desk with the largest array of Southwestern treasures and fingered some.

"For all the regression modeling we did, we never did establish the characteristics or variables for those most likely to respond to EthosBot therapy versus those not. All the years of clinical trials ... we should have been able to identify some predictors regarding who with anxiety or depression would respond to Ethos. Yet, we didn't." He cleared his throat and rubbed his forehead.

"Cali, my dear, come here. Find some treasures that speak to you and take them with you. My gift."

"Dr. Rane, that's so generous. They all mean so much to you."

"Indeed. I'm not getting any younger though, and something tells me a couple of these artistic creations belong in your hands."

She looked at Dr. Rane and found him gazing at the collection of Southwest Native American memorabilia. Cali touched two stone sculptures. One was a three-inch gray onyx horse with a mix of intriguing striations. It was adorned with tiny turquoise stone eyes and a cinch of several stones affixed with jute. *Sabino.*

Then, she hovered over a similarly sized, lavender jade Indian woman figurine bedecked with turquoise and coral jewelry. *Is this me?*

Finally, she could not resist a pottery sculpture of a storyteller. Black and cinnamon paint depicted soft hair, gentle faces, and Indian clothing. Two children were nestled in the storyteller's arms. *My mom. Sage. Me and Kalen as kids.*

Dr. Rane smiled broadly. "They're meant for you. And, yes, the storyteller is your mother."

Cali had to wipe a few tears away. Dr. Rane gently guided her back toward the leather chairs.

"Now, cue that tablet of yours and let's go through your notes. I'll tell you what you can quote me on, and the rest will need to remain simple allusion or anonymous in your exposé."

When they'd finished, Cali thanked him profusely for his time and information. She held the three treasures next to her heart, and with a few more tears, she retreated to the front door.

"Have you ever been to the hacienda? My mom would love to see you again, and my dad, Bayani, makes authentic fire-roasted tamales. You should come sometime. We'd all love it."

Turning reserved, he said, "Oh, I don't know if your mom wants to see an old goat like me rising from her past."

"You're not old. You're a worldly gentleman, and my mother could not have done her job without you. You made an incredible difference during the early years of the biotechnology. What you contributed to the Ethos clinical trials was no small feat either. Oh, come to the ranch ... yes, think about it. I'll call or send a message with an invitation."

He genuinely laughed at her simplicity, forthrightness, and caring. "Cali, be safe, and do say hello to your mother."

Cali was about to step through the doorway when she abruptly turned and gave Dr. Rane a hug.

He watched as she boarded the Float vehicle. As he closed the front door, he turned and faced the interior of his modern but stuffed-with-unique-artifacts home.

I'm alone though. Her departure makes me feel more … alone. He rubbed his forehead, then his face. He felt depression descend and distractedly rubbed his chest. He didn't believe he'd make it through the night. If it's my time, so be it. As the ancient ones would say at an intuitive time, it's a good day to pass to the next world.

♦

Cali returned home and spying Carson near the barn, she strode toward him. Feeling content from her interview with Dr. Rane, she wanted to be outdoors.

"Hey, babe. How'd it go?" Although he wanted to greet her with a kiss, he decided it best to keep his actions suitable for the work environment, but with endearing words.

"It was easier to talk to him than I thought. His history with the bots is so amazing. I wondered if my exposé project would seem trite to him. As hoped, he shared quite a few details that I can use as a stand-alone narrative and to augment whatever Kalen and Zia uncover with trial volunteers. Carson, he was so kind."

Trying to decide if she wanted to get in a quick ride, Cali played with Sabino's soft muzzle. "Is Kalen back from class yet? Mom home from work? I need to tell her about Dr. Rane."

"Have not seen Kalen yet, but your mom came home early. Hey, how did it go the other day with you and Kalen and Uncle Cy at FSPA?"

Cali turned momentarily pensive and tilted her head at Carson. "Wait. How'd you know we were taken to FSPA headquarters? Kalen and I decided not to say anything until all the tryst & schemers met together. I'm sure my father didn't mention anything. It was a Saturday. We could have gone anywhere with our uncle."

Carson's mouth tightened, he puffed out a breath, and ran his hand through his hair. To Cali, it was blatant stalling. He was hiding something.

Cali whispered, "It was you. You told Uncle Cy about Project Paint." Seeing his reaction, she became vehement. "Carson, what, what were you thinking? Wait, that's why you're not posting at all. You pretend to give this big brother advice but leave all the nitty-gritty work to the rest of us."

She snapped her fingers and shook her hand. "That's why I felt funny the other day about some of your comments. It was as if you knew something you shouldn't."

Carson went to grab Cali's hand and she pulled away. Sabino nickered and threw her head up at the dissension between the two humans.

"Cal, I ... I have your best interest at heart. I know how angry you are about Ethos and the Earth event. As the schemers got heavier into plotting, I thought of Uncle Cy. He's in a perfect position to watch over you. Make sure you don't do anything you'll regret. I told him just enough about Project Paint so he could help if need be. He promised he would only use the information to keep you safe and not interfere with the schemers.

"Cal, it was harmless and meant to protect you. You're heading to the university next year, and I don't want anything to change that for you."

As Carson spoke, Cali's face became rosy and contorted with frustration. Her mouth opened trying to find words that didn't come. As she struggled to make sense of what she'd just heard, Sabino nudged her shoulder.

"You ... you violated my trust ... the trust of the tryst

& schemers. I thought we loved one another, but true love doesn't involve back room dealing and feigned protection. Protection from what exactly? … And how … how dare you believe that you need to watch over my actions and control what my future might be."

Cal's voice grew louder as she grew increasingly irate. Nearby, some of the barn hands studied the pair wondering if they would need to intervene.

"We're done, Carson."

"Cal, wait." He grabbed her arm, so he could continue the dialogue and make a case for the action he took.

"Let go. Leave me alone. I said, we're done, and I mean it." As she ran up to the hacienda courtyard, Bayani approached Carson.

The two stared at one another. Carson looked angry and hurt. He simply shook his head and said nothing. *Failed attempt,* he telepathed to no one in particular.

Still facing Carson, Bayani placed one boot on a low beam of a nearby post and rail fence. Leaning on the top rail with his forearms, he adjusted his cowboy hat. Bayani was quiet. He waited.

Finally, Carson turned and finding his trusty quarter horse, Bandit, he saddled up in haste. He was adjusting the bridle when Bayani stood next to him.

"Carson, probably not a good time to ride. It'll be dark soon, and best if you're not out there alone."

Carson bent his head clearly pondering how to reply. "Bayani, I love Cali, I love your daughter. You know that. I'd never hurt her. I believe Uncle Cy, Agent Desai was the right person to keep an eye on her and her friends. I've been nothing but a gentleman with her … no matter how much opportunity there's been to be more amorous. I respect her, and I respect you and your wife."

With long determined strides, he led his horse to the gate and mounted.

Bayani was on his heels. "Carson!"

"No. Cali's right to be upset. I should have trusted she would do the right thing when it came down to it. I have no right to pretend to protect her future ... Cal's her own person. It's why ... it's why I love her." In a show of respect, he tipped his hat at Bayani saying, "Now, I've gotta ride."

"Carson. Carson, wait!"

Bayani's words were lost on the early evening wind being churned up by the change in temperature from warm desert day to chilly desert night. More failed attempts. Another full moon on the rise ...

Chapter 10

FISSURES

Inside the main casa, Cali blubbered with her mother over the end of romance. She cried freely into Sage's arms. "Mom, I still love him. What's wrong me? I hate that he went behind my back and all my friends. Project Crazy Paint created protected space for us to make a difference. A difference in how Ethos moves forward or not … and now it's been invaded."

Cali held no pretense that her mother was unaware of the tryst & schemers. Surely, her mother knew. Sage was an Adept.

"First of all, of course you still love him. You've been together for a year with so few disagreements. Unless it's the ultimate betrayal between two in a committed relationship, love doesn't stop or fade at the first stumble … In this very minute when you say you still love him, that's a good thing. Your love is credible. It has meaning. For both of you."

Sage allowed Cali to pull back from the embrace and wipe away tears.

"Secondly, I understand why this feels like betrayal. He took it upon himself to tell someone outside your motley group of schemers." Sage couldn't help but smirk endearingly as she eyed Cali.

In response, Cali pursed her lips in irritation. "You genuinely know about us schemers?"

Sighing with a soft smile, Sage merely raised her eyebrows at the last query. Instead, she addressed the current drama.

"On the other hand, Carson's intentions were sincere. Some would say smart even. If there was someone to tell, to keep you and your clandestine group safe ... Uncle Cy is the perfect 'go to' guy. He's your uncle and a federal agent with the knowledge and means to protect you. Uncle Cyprus would never invade your privacy or compromise you, Kalen, or your friends in any manner. I'm certain Carson sees that in your uncle. Now, was it an action Carson should have taken? Was it wise? It's not for me to say."

"Another side to the story," Cali conceded. She took a seat in one of the bar height equipale chairs normally snugged up against the kitchen island. "I get it, Mom. It kinda makes me feel better, but kinda not."

Spoken in true teen fashion. Sage sighed again and squeezed Cali's hand.

"Can I change the subject, sweetie? How did it go with Dr. Rane?"

The change in topic turned Cali cautiously enlivened. She relayed how fondly he recalled his time working with Sage and the bot-teamers. She described some of what they discussed and promised to give her mom a chance to read the article before posting. After all, her mom's workplace would be at the forefront. Too, her mother had been instrumental in hooking her up with Dr. Rane.

"Thanks for recommending him, Mom. He was honest, insightful, and it gave me a better perspective on Ethos and the clinical trials. I understand why you work so hard. Although the Earth event was tragic, you can't adamantly decide to crush the EthosBot. Years of scientific work and meager successes were tantalizing enough to not let go ..."

At the breakthrough, the compassion, Sage smiled at her daughter.

"Oh, look what treasures he gave me. From all the cherished Southwestern artistry in his library, he asked me to find what drew me in." Cali pulled the onyx horse, lavender jade Indian woman figurine, and storyteller from her large bag.

"Dr. Rane gave these up? They're beautiful! Cal, he must have seen something very special in you, honey."

"This one is for you — the storyteller. I told him it was you ... my mother, Sage."

Now, it was Sage's turn to tear up. "I see you found Sabino and ... you found yourself."

"Yup, Mom, I found myself. I'm as strong as stone." She laid her hand atop her mother's and gently squeezed. "Mom, the other night with the extended family ... my accusations, anger ..."

"Let it go. Families are allowed to get angry and disagree with one another over serious deeds and notions. Within these walls and whenever family is beside you, be honest, speak your mind, your truth. Always."

The tender moment was disturbed by Cali's personal device. Gabe sent a 'see you soon'. "Oh right, Gabe."

Her mother simply held up her hands in surrender, as if to say, 'don't tell me'.

Cali laughed. "It's a good time to run to Gabe. It's a really, really bad time to run to Gabe."

"Hhhmmm ... well said, my dear daughter. Let me know if you do go out. I have a feeling the romantic drama is just beginning."

Sage had to let her daughter figure this out on her own. If she asked for advice, fine. Otherwise, Cali was off to college next year, and she'd either fostered good judgment or not. Sage sure as heck knew mistakes were part of the life journey, not crafted just for youth. Hopefully, the good sense instilled at home resulted in formative mishaps, not irreversible radical errors.

Cali eyed her mom. Hard to believe the famous Sage was a teenager once, an esteemed bot-teamer and eco-terrorist rebel. If her mom was indeed all that, Cali's future was destined to be a roller coaster ride.

♦

It began with a rush of wind through treetops, accelerating in seconds, and putting Carson on notice. Uncharacteristically, his horse, Bandit, pulled up short and sidestepped. The gust quickened becoming thunderous. Simultaneously, he felt an electrifying painful skin and muscle sensation. It was the vertigo that startled and Bandit's cursory rearing that forced action.

Carson dismounted in haste. His boots barely hit the ground when the whirlwind hit forcefully. He pulled Bandit's face into his chest and bent over to shield them both from sand and debris. As the wind dwindled and the air cleared, that's when Carson spied the fissure that paralleled his path home.

"Bandit," he spoke aloud, "appreciate the warning, buddy. You only rear with your herd mates — never with me on your back. So, I knew whatever was coming was bad. If the ground had split under a full gallop, it could have been lethal for us."

In the instant fear of knowing what tragedy the two

of them had fortunately avoided, Carson trembled. Flight or fight adrenaline didn't help the fear or shaking either.

The earth fissure frightened Carson. From his position on unsteady legs, it was one to five feet across as it zigzagged behind and in front of him, roughly parallel to the trail, and then veering west. As he gazed across the landscape in waning daylight, discerning additional cracked and sunken areas was difficult.

Dusk had descended as he rode the trail further and further out to free his mind from the unsettled affair with Cali. The ride had indeed cleared his head, but now he faced another situation. Riding in the dark of night was not a concern. Never ideal, but Carson had done it countless times over the years out of necessity. Now, uncharted ground beneath his and Bandit's feet was alarming — especially if additional seismic activity occurred.

Still holding the reins, he sank to his knees. His thoughts jumbled. It's getting darker by the minute, and there may not be enough light to judge the crevasse and reliability of the ground as we head back to the ranch. Once up, the full moon may give us enough light. ... My phone sits on a post rail near a stall. I should telepath Bayani. No, one of the ranch hands instead.

In a feeble attempt to thought transfer, Carson realized telepathy was stymied by an apparent second round of a creepy electrified tempest. A second storm but this time with visible seismic effects, he reasoned. No one should have to rescue me ...

Darn it all. Bayani pleaded not to ride in my state of mind. Cali. Where's Cali? Is she okay or did she grab Sabino and follow me? No, she's rightfully angry. I'm dead in the water with her ...

Bandit gently nudged his distraught rider who was

deeply contemplating the situation. *We walk. Side by side. What you cannot sense beneath our feet, I can.*

You got it, Bandit, my boy.

With the assurance of his steed, Carson began the long walk home. He didn't even hold the reins and lead. Bandit knew best. Together, on hoof and foot, they navigated new landscape.

♦

Gabe greeted Cali with a soft kiss on the cheek that reverberated to her toes. From the brief brush of his lips, fragrant notes of sandalwood, cardamom, and aquatic filled her senses.

She'd chosen an oversized blouse, a tight thigh-length skirt and new sporty shoes. A fun silky soft sweater kept the chill away.

Gabe was taller than her, and she liked that. He was dressed casually in a T-shirt and jeans with a chocolate brown leather jacket. His slender build was toned and athletic, and she wondered what he did to create those muscular arms. Was it due to being a medic or his recreational pursuits? His medium brown, sun-streaked hair reminded Cali of a surfer look, but Gabe's locks were neat and shorter on the side, touching his T-shirt at the nape of his neck. Just like the first day she met him, she thought he was handsomely cute. Carson was handsome too but rugged.

They'd decided on a *T-Scape* university haunt. It was an eclectic restaurant and bar with indoor and outdoor cozy seating for couples or smaller groups, and larger tables with benches for the larger likely rowdy crowd.

Conversation came effortlessly. It felt as if there wasn't enough time to get it all in. They were getting to know one another, and yet, it felt as if they already knew the other. Perhaps, a meant-to-be soul connection brought together by the EthosBot and activists.

"What drew you to become a medic? Healthcare professionals in your family?"

"Both parents are in healthcare. When the profession was upended by BioBots healing everyone, they floundered. Their patience and insight into charting a modified career helped me figure out what I wanted to do. Over time, the profession found other ways to adapt to the altered care paradigm, and I found my way to majoring in medicine.

"I enjoy being a medic, but my goal is to work at *T-Care*. Rather than running around in a vehicle never knowing what will be encountered, I'd rather be in one place with others where I can treat people as urgent or emergency cases. There's high demand for licensed providers or physicians who know how to intertwine aspects of former care with BioBot technologies. At least for now, people still need to be stitched up — as you well know from personal experience.

"The bots originally functioned as super pharmaceutical agents, but did you know? Now, there's a series of bots involved in acute mending of things such as fractures and wounds. Cutting edge stuff ..."

"No, I didn't know that. Thought mainstream bot therapy was it — chewable, skin patch, or embedded chip, all of which take time to spin healing effects. Interesting what you describe on the horizon. Next time, a bot could stitch me up?"

Gabe nodded, "Your famous mom hasn't told you about the new wave of BioBots?"

"My mother has issues of work confidentiality. To be honest, the team she's worked on for decades continually morphs and expands as the biotech seems to take on a life of its own. She can only be involved in so much."

Looking down, Cali twirled the straw in her drink and knitted her eyebrows in concern. "Over time, I believe she's become disengaged ... almost apathetic or maybe worn down. Sometimes, I think she is in a daze, simply moving through the day without the purpose she used to have."

Running her hand through one side of her hair, Cali sat up straighter. "You know, I've not expressed this to anyone else until now. It feels deeply personal. I apologize ... feel as if I betrayed my mother." Nervously, she smiled and shook her head.

"Hey, it's fine. What you tell me goes nowhere. Remember, I'm a medic and soon to be a physician — of some type, I hope. My coworkers and I may entertain with general stories about our workday, but we never reveal anything of import."

They jabbered more about families, social upheaval, and even reminisced about the campus riot that brought them together. Soon the conversation turned to activities of fun and escapism.

"I know you and your brother ride regularly, and you love cross-country jumps. I follow your social posts about equine telepathy and bareback riding with no bridle. Quite remarkable."

"Growing up at the hacienda, I was born to ride. Telepathic connection with animals amplified the desire and skill. Sabino, all our horses, our dogs are everything to me."

"Any room for a boyfriend?" Seeing Cali smile and blush was all the confirmation he needed. He paused a beat and continued. "I run mostly. It clears my mind. I do throw grass hay and alfalfa bales at a nearby barn a few days a week. In return, I can ride their horses."

"You've been holding out on me! You ride too? Now I understand those biceps — bucking hay will do it." Unguarded, the comment referring to Gabe's upper body strength slid into conversation. Cali quickly regretted it and added, "We should ride sometime."

Suddenly, restaurant lighting flickered, and barely perceptible, the floor beneath their table rolled. Simultaneously feeling a whole-body tingling sensation and hearing a distinct electrical buzz, Cali and Gabe froze and stared at one another.

"Another Earth event," Cali murmured just loud enough for Gabe to hear. "If it emanated from *TIA* here on the *T-Scape* campus, it's gonna be worse as the vibrations expand outward. The hacienda! The animals again ..."

Gabe had no time to reply when both of their phones sounded alerts.

Cali studied the succinct message on her phone from her father. 'Cal, another tempest here. Are you okay?'

"Oh no, Gabe. It did hit the ranch."

She replied to her dad. 'At a restaurant on campus. Ground quake, electrification, but okay.' *Wow, strange phones working this time. Wonder if I can telepath ...*

'Cal, please come. Ground fissures this time. Carson left on Bandit after disagreement. He's not back. It's dark. Fissures on horseback trouble. Going after him with Kalen. Stay with your mother.'

'Dad, don't go. Please. Kalen and I will go after Carson.' The text message blinked 'aborted'.

"Had phone capabilities, but now it's out."

"Mine too," Gabe asserted.

"I've gotta go, Gabe. This Earth event produced ground fissures! The rolling earthquake here became amplified further out." Cali was shaking now. "Carson. He's out there. On the trail. In the dark with ravines! Bandit … they could both be injured." Thinking the worst of a fallen rider and broken leg on Bandit, she bit her lip and grabbed her sweater.

Gabe picked up his leather jacket and reached for Cali's arm. "I'm going with you. I can follow you home and ride out too. Cali, we'll find Carson."

In the desperate moment, Cali didn't have the emotional mindset to decline Gabe's offer. As she drove in haste in the Float toward home, she kicked herself for not insisting Gabe stay out of this drama.

Whatever was going to happen tonight with Carson was her own doing. *I'm sorry, Carson. I should have tried to understand your motivation. It was love. Misplaced maybe. But I should have …* She wiped tears away knowing the telepathed message was going nowhere in the ethereal mayhem.

Cali ignored the local speed limit. Let someone try to stop me from getting to Carson, she thought.

She parked the Float as close as she could to the barn and then ran. Kalen was saddled up with supplies and already mounted on Kona. Bayani was ready to mount Dakota when Cali, breathless, firmly placed a hand on her father's shoulder. "Dad, no. Let Kalen and I go. It's too much for you."

Gabe was right on Cali's tail. "Mr. Casander, Sir. I'm Gabe, a friend of Cali's. I'm a rider and a medic. I've got a foldup backboard that I can take with me … on any horse you give me … It could come in handy if Carson's got a fractured leg or …" He stopped. The point was taken. Cali was now pale, and her father appeared forlorn.

After a few minutes, Bayani acquiesced reluctantly. Gabe's medic skills could be critical if Carson was injured.

The board he described was well known. It was a lightweight, puzzle-piece wonder of interlocking segments that could be adjusted to fit adults and children, backs, legs, arms, necks — whatever body part required stabilizing in the field.

It was decided too that Gabe ride Dakota. Not witnessing Gabe's riding acumen meant giving him a horse that would assuredly carry him no matter the circumstance. Being supremely even-keeled, Dakota was the perfect fit in the moment.

Cali was forced to remain behind with her parents. She watched as Kalen and Gabe took off with reflective gear and low illuminators clipped to tack. At a very modest pace, they agreed to follow the trail as best as they could while giving a wide berth to zigzagging crevasses. The full moon was high now casting eerie light and shadow.

Since they knew Carson's phone was uselessly perched on a post rail, Cali's role was to keep trying to contact him with telepathic messages. Kalen and Gabe promised to stay in touch with thought transference when the air cleared for telepathy to work. Disruption of the EMF was likely the culprit yet again.

Two of the ranch hands ignited nearby firepits. It was to warm those standing watch, as well as provide a beacon to those roaming the darkness beyond.

Sage handed Cali pants and a coat. The night chill would only grow, and a short skirt and sweater wouldn't cut the hours ahead nor the potential demands of helping any wounded. Appreciative, Cali scooted to an open stall and unabashedly changed from skirt to pants.

Going from chair to pacing and back again, Cali telepathed sporadically hoping to breakthrough. She bounced between human and horse thought transference.

Carson, where are you? Carson, talk to me. We see the ground fissures. We're coming for you. Tell us where you are on the trail.

Bandit ... Bandit ... Dakota and Kona are looking for you ... barn buddies ... Kalen's coming.

After almost an hour, the air and energy fields cleared. It began with a light breeze followed by the yips of *Coyote*. The packs signaled a return to normal.

Cal! Foot, leg jammed into a fissure. Shin beat up. Gosh darn, the pain ... Bandit's okay, right beside me.

Carson, can you tell where you are on the trail? Kalen and Gabe have gotta be close. They've been looking for you.

Lights, I see their lights. Bandit's nickering to them. I hope ... I think ... they see me. I've been struggling to break free ... shooting pain.

In haste, Cali telepathed her brother and Gabe simultaneously. *Bandit should be nickering to you. Do you hear him? Carson says his leg is stuck in a fissure.*

Within minutes, contact was made. Although Carson had walked beside his trusty steed carefully assessing every step with the aid of moonlight, an unseen rift, just the right size to capture boot and leg, spun tragedy.

Kalen and Gabe found Carson quite exhausted from the push-pull of trying to dislodge his lower leg by digging at surrounding soil. A few rock shards lay nearby, and his leather riding gloves were shredded.

Too, a lariat was positioned around Carson's upper body with the end of the rope landing near Bandit. He'd obviously tried to have Bandit pull him out.

Seeing Carson physically compromised shook Kalen. After all, Carson had been Kalen's big brother as he grew up on the ranch. Following Carson around like a shadow, Kalen had learned as much from Carson as he had from his father, Bayani.

Kalen and Gabe assessed the situation. The desert soil and rock could be nasty to work or reshape. Strangely, soil eroded from sandstone buttes could appear as sugar-fine sand, spanning trails and creating dunes. It all depended on the composition of rock layers. Or if one moved a few miles in another direction, the rock and soil type changed acting like concrete against a shovel. In this spot, the unforgiving limestone and conglomerate were nearly impossible to dig, and the dark of night only augmented the challenge.

Creatively, they considered cutting through Carson's leather boot to release his foot. Due to the trauma and possible tibial fracture though, the swelling of his entire lower leg and foot made boot removal and the hope of sliding his foot out extremely remote. So, taking turns, they dug with the shovel that Kalen had thoughtfully included with the rescue supplies.

While Kalen began the tedious excavation, Gabe put his medic skills and kit to good use. Judging Carson to be in early-stage shock and dehydrated, he gave him mineral-infused water. Gabe was also able to squeeze an ice pack alongside Carson's shin, which after a few minutes, provided some relief. Gabe recommended an analgesic injection that Carson gratefully accepted.

"Alleviating the pain will help calm you, especially since digging you out will take a bit. Plus, it'll take time to ride back." It hadn't taken much convincing, and once the injection took effect, Carson's demeanor improved.

With partial alleviation of pain and weakness, Carson turned falteringly congenial. "You're the medic we met the other night in town. You saved Cali and her mom from the campus riot. Lucky you're here."

Gabe was uncertain what to say, so instead avoided the

concept of how any luck brought him here tonight. "Kalen, my turn to work the shovel."

Kalen ran the back of his hand across his forehead, and willingly handed over digging responsibility.

"I hope I can ride back, guys," Carson winced as they dug around his leg.

"No worries, bro," Kalen chuckled weakly, somewhat breathless from working the soil. "We'll figure this out … rescue equipment inside those saddlebags … hang in there with us."

Gabe added nothing more to the conversation, but instead pondered the awkward turn of events. From a date with Cali to digging out Carson — who clearly showed his caring for her when they met at the Mexican restaurant. To boot, digging out her beau or *a* beau with her brother. Regardless of the odd situation, he was glad to help. It was what he did, what he loved.

After twenty minutes of vigorous digging by Kalen and Gabe, the rocky earth released its hold on Carson's lower leg. With Carson seated on firm ground and legs extended, they tore open the left leg of his jeans revealing the severity of the injury. From the knee down, the lower leg was significantly discolored and swollen. Without a radiographic image, Gabe could only guess the type of fracture. The boot was likely acting as a tourniquet on the foot keeping the fluid at the shin area.

Gabe telepathed to Kalen, *I don't know if we cut the boot off or not. It's a judgment call.* Gabe shook his head in aggravation, as he wished he knew the best thing to do in this situation.

Let's do the required and get him outta here, Kalen replied.

"We're gonna ice and stabilize just below the knee,"

Gabe explained breathing in deeply. "I'm afraid to stabilize the knee area too, as we've got to get you in the saddle. If there is any way that we can elevate your leg while you're riding, we need to try. To do that, you may need to bend your knee. Too, you may need the flexibility of your knee for balance in the saddle — especially without use of a stirrup."

"I can ride without stirrups. Being able to bend my knee, just sounds more comfortable. To get me up, Bandit can fold his legs, so I can climb into the saddle. Then you guys can fiddle with elevating my leg, or I say, let's just get a move on. My leg's not getting any prettier lookin'."

It was evident Carson was putting on a brave face — a face that was now more pale than several minutes ago and damp despite the chilly night air.

"Guys, we'll use the lariat to partially string up the left leg to the saddle horn," Kalen offered. "I'll lead us out of here. Gabe, you follow Carson. Bring up the rear. Stick to a line behind me, as Kona and I will pick out the trail ahead."

With that final bit of strategizing, Carson's leg was bandaged, bound, and artfully slung against the side of Bandit. The slightly bent leg was awkwardly but effectively elevated to prevent the unchecked influx of fluid to the injury.

For field medicine, it's the best we can do, Kalen and Gabe agreed.

Kona found sturdy ground, keeping a bright walk to return to the ranch in haste but without misstep. *The warm fire of the hacienda is not far ahead,* Kona relayed to his rider.

Assured by Kona, Kalen allowed his thoughts to wander, and wander they did. Within a few short weeks, two rescues involving those for whom I care so much. Tryst & schemers, twists & fissures in the ground. Carson and Gabe with Cali. More tryst and fissure ... So much unknown.

Relationships. EthosBot … Zia. I need Zia. I need time with Aunt Kehlani — her peaceful, *knowing* way …

The three riders were all lost in their own mind meanderings. Before long, hacienda firelight beckoned.

Cali watched the return of the men she loved.

The ranch hands sprang into action releasing the lariat holding Carson's leg, as Cali ran to his side and grabbed his hand. "Carson," was all she could muster as she gazed into his eyes. He simply squeezed her hand. He felt lightheaded and nearly fell into the arms of his fellow ranchers. They hustled him to a waiting vehicle.

Cali bit her lip and watched. Then she moved alongside the Float where Carson was lying flat with eyes closed. She reached for his arm, "I'll be there at *T-Care* as quickly as I can. Carson. I … I'm here, honey."

As the Float hovered away, Kalen slid next to his sister. Seeing tears in her eyes for Carson, he pontificated, "Tears are not meant for Carson or anyone else. They're meant for you, Cali. Fix this. Choose or at least be clear about what you want from each of them." Kalen jostled his shoulder against Cali as if to say, 'I love you anyway'.

Kalen said nothing more and walked away. Even though it was late, he wanted to see Zia.

Gabe watched as Cali interacted with Carson and then her brother. He felt suddenly alone.

As Gabe quietly retreated to his vehicle, Bayani gave a shout and hurried over to Gabe before he departed. "Thanks for your help. You were right. You were the right man for the job tonight. Thanks for working with Kalen to bring Carson back."

"Glad I could help. Tell Cali goodnight."

Cali caught Gabe speaking with her father, and she walked toward them.

"Hhhmmm … tell her yourself." Bayani smiled at Gabe. Teens and trysts, he thought to himself. Getting too old for all this.

Unsure how to be with Gabe in the moment, Cali fisted her hand to her lips and studied Gabe for any nonverbal cue. Gabe turned to get in his vehicle.

"Wait, Gabe." Cali offered a hug, but Gabe weakly placed just one arm around her waist as she embraced his shoulders. "Thanks for rescuing Carson. I … I enjoyed our time tonight … sorry this happened."

"Cali, you've got some things to sort out. I like you a lot. Figure out Carson first." With that, he climbed into his Float vehicle and ramped up hover mode.

Cali stepped back. Fissure. Maybe more than one.

♦

A few hours later … patio doors still ajar, a steady late-night breeze streamed through the Rane library. Papers were strewn and blown against shelves. A still, breathless form lay slumped in a leather chair. *Coyote* howled.

Chapter 11

FREAKING ETHOS

"Ethos freaking changed them." Zia had a forthright expressive manner, and this was certainly not a time to hold back. "Kalen, almost every single trial volunteer we've interviewed has talked about fundamental changes in who they are, what they like, don't like, believe, don't believe. Getting this out will have huge repercussions."

While Cali had been with Dr. Rane getting insider details concerning how the clinical EthosBot trials were conducted, Zia and Kalen were entrenched for several days with interviews. With Nate's help, they secured another quiet out-of-way university location to conduct private conversations with trial volunteers. For about two to three hours on four consecutive evenings, they'd diligently gone through prescribed questions. After hours of talking and listening, forty EthosBot cases had shared their experiences.

Kalen and Zia were seated at a concrete desk in the tryst & schemers Project Paint hideaway. The screen with the data summary from the trial volunteers was posted neatly in front of them. Logistic regression models show-cased a mix and match of variables or conditions and the consequential prediction for improvement or outright cure of anxiety and depression. Thankfully, Zane and Nate had set up potential models, and Kalen and Zia simply had to select the data elements, and voilà, the software churned out lovely statistics.

Of note, their data was based entirely on patient or individual case self-report, not a medical record. Too, as in all public health and clinical data related to turamali anything, the data was subject to other limitations as well — such as *perceived* cure or improvement and to what degree. Still the discovery held profound meaning.

Kalen sighed heavily. "It's what we anticipated from just listening to the Ethos trial cases. Recovery from anxiety and/or depression seems moot, unimportant compared to what Ethos wrought instead. Right, Z, this is frightening and staggering. Reporting this will have social repercussions we can only imagine. We've got to pull the tryst & schemers together right away before we start the media firestorm."

Thus, the following evening the schemers were once again tucked in at their secretive gathering place. Being curious about what the trial data revealed via their creative regression model manipulations, Zane and Nate pulled up the statistical models immediately upon joining the gathering.

In awe, Zane whispered a few expletives. Taking a more serious note, Nate became visibly restless after studying the results of the trial cases.

"This can't be. When people discover … this is bigger than any scandal, tragedy … the ethics of Ethos … my god!" Nate paced and wrung his hands as he mumbled.

Seeing his distress, both Zane and Zia offered comfort. Zane gently shook Nate's shoulders. Placing his cheek and lips near Nate's ear, he spoke in barely audible words to his dear friend. With a gentle ease, Zia smoothed her hand down one of Nate's arms, and then taking his hand, she held it firmly between hers. Centering herself, she allowed calming vibrations to emanate from her to Nate.

In mere seconds, Nate succumbed to the consolation. Slightly embarrassed even among his closest companions, Nate quickly hugged Zia, then took up a seat distant from the screen with the ominous data. Zane joined him on an adjacent chair.

Lastly, Carson and Cali arrived together securing the door firmly behind them. Carson wore a walking boot which was barely discernable beneath his comfy loose-fitting pants. Materials technology had come a long way over the past decade. Although thin and lightweight, the foreign object on his leg was still clearly a nuisance, as Carson winced and appeared aggravated by the handicap. Barely two days had gone by, thus pain and discomfort remained evident. After all, the Radiance BioBot took time to forge healing magic.

Carson and Cali plopped themselves on an oversized chair, and Kalen positioned an ottoman beneath Carson's gimpy leg. Over time, Nate had slowly acquired overstuffed chairs from around the building to make the schemers' hideaway congenial and comfy. Fortuitously, an ottoman had been spirited away from another lounge.

It was difficult to tell what was going on between the two trysters, but Carson purposefully, albeit nonchalantly, bumped and rubbed his knee against Cali's leg. He was trying, hoping. Cali was undecided but fell into the role she'd come to know so well over the past year with her beau.

Having called the urgent gathering, Kalen and Zia were excited and anxious to share their findings. They perched together on a wood bench with thick cushions. They both leaned forward, and Kalen jostled Zia nodding to her, 'you go first'.

"The devious bot we bantered about a few weeks ago ... It's far worse than we imagined. At that time, we saw what it or something related to it could reap. The Earth event was tragic, but we only speculated about what the EthosBot could do to the human psyche. Forty trial volunteers later, we know.

"First, it was truly serendipitous we met the small group commiserating at the restaurant. They willingly offered to contact other cases involved in the trials. In a very short time, Kalen and I were able to garner the support of many who were eager to talk about their experience. We heard the same thematic consequence from every ... single ... case. Not just a trend or risk for some side effect. Every person became a new, different person with their customized embedded EthosBot."

"Z, what exactly are you saying?" Cali probed. She had an idea, but since the results were only revealed in the last day, Kalen and Zia had committed to keeping a lid on the outcome data until all the schemers could review the results together and make a group decision. Too, if the findings were that profound, it would be a plunge into social maelstrom when reported to the world.

"Ethos changed them. Fundamentally, as in who they are." The characteristic Zia who held a comical bent, although different than her brother Zane, was now dramatically serious. "Preferences, opinions, patterns of thinking, choices, feelings, what they now want to do in life ... It's as if EthosBot may have alleviated the anxiety or depression but replaced it with new brain wiring."

"We specifically asked about perceived changes in personality, moods, choices," Kalen chimed in. "Get this. Political and religious ideologies changed. If someone espoused economic nationalism, they turned to economic liberalism. Those supporting corporatism turned to socialism.

"Religiously, some converted from one faith to another — within related faiths or moving to an entirely different world belief system. Interestingly, many simply left their former faith behind and took on a sort of world spiritualism ... described as a pervasive mental and emotional peace as if they were simply moving between worlds, going from one vibrational portal to another, with or without their physical body. Eerily, this world spiritualism was described similarly by just about every trial volunteer whether they maintained their pre-EthosBot religious affiliation or not. Descriptions were vague and well, ethereal. Ethotic, if there could be such a descriptor."

"Ethotic," Cali murmured tilting her head. The group turned attention to Cali as her voice remained soft. "EthosBot creating ethoism or an ethotic state? Are those even real words? Way weird, guys."

After a brief pause to let the first wave of news settle, Zia picked up the dialogue. "Crystal type, clinical category of anxiety or depression — none of it was associated with changes in political, social, or religious ideologic beliefs. No demographic associations either, such as age, gender, career. It simply appeared Ethos changed people. Everyone ... that's every volunteer we interviewed ... experienced this world spiritualism or ethotic state."

"There's more," Kalen continued. "Recreational activities changed. Runners and hikers took up group sports and vice versa. Cases explained they suddenly couldn't stand running or hiking. It felt too separate and alone. They felt compelled to join a team sport. Or again, vice versa. Food choices and nutrition modified. Ethnic foods they had formerly loved became boring, or the vegetarian Earth-friendly diet they'd consumed for years turned tasteless."

Moving away from Kalen, Zia stood and leaned against the wall near a window. She flipped off her sandals to feel the cold concrete beneath her feet. Momentarily lost in thought, she appeared to study her sparkly toenail polish. She ran her hand through her freeform wavy bob.

Zia glanced around at her companions. "What we just elaborated is merely a backdrop. I mean, the big picture is the Ethos trial cases feel and act like different people now. Ethos altered the fundamental way that neurons, synapses, and neurotransmitters all synch together ... altering desire, intention, will, and thus forging divergent thought, choice ... fabricating unfamiliar alternative personality, demeanor."

Then to get the schemers full attention, she whispered with a vehemence and drama only Z could pull off. "Ethos, the devious little BioBot freaking changed people. No one, no one has reported this. Nothing in company updates, nor even peer-reviewed published medical articles."

"We report this then? As planned?" Nate was tentative.

"Yo, yes, brothers and sisters, fellow tryst & schemers, absolutely yes." Zaner was animated and shifted his position on the chair. "After the Earth event, this is exactly the dirt and scary revelation we believed we'd find. I say, Zia and Kalen, your work was stellar with the trial cases, and the data say it all. Guys, we need to get this out. Now."

Nate was a bit pale, biting his lower lip and shifting uneasily in his chair. Suddenly, feeling kinship with Zia, he joined her and stood against the wall. He too needed to feel the cold against his skin. Dropping the back of his head against the cool surface, he kicked off his Jesus-style sandals to feel the concrete chill. Anything to alleviate the vertigo and restore his normal pragmatic academic focus.

Then as he spoke, Nate slumped to the floor lamenting, "What will happen when we report this? It's not supposition, theory, storytelling, social blithering. We've collected clinical data and created statistical models that don't lie. Sure, someone can always poke holes in this or that study limitation, but the results stand. As Z says, people are freaking altered. This is huge for what happens next when the world finds out. Ethos *is* devious. Now, we know."

In twin synch, Cali and Kalen spoke together, "Truth. Pandemonium."

"We'll need to do this strategically as if we're composing a typical science-based paper ... with balance, fairness." Kalen confirmed.

"The facts, the data stand for themselves. No drama, no baseless claims." Cali concurred. "Let the media and social networks interpret and takeoff with our findings."

With her last statement, Cali turned to study Carson's expression. Then she added, "We need to provide the data and whatever narrative we compose to Uncle Cy and my mom. That's before we post publicly. It's the right thing to do. And, we sort of committed to that."

"What? When?" Zia was surprised and confused by the new tack to have outsiders review their postings in advance. She stared at Cali and then Kalen.

Kalen sighed heavily. "This past Saturday, Cal and I got pulled into FSPA headquarters. We were asked about Project Paint ... TripleTempest, DustDevil."

"Ouch, man! Did they ask about Spook?" Zane was quick to respond to the unexpected intrusion into their scheming.

"Oh, please don't tell me they know where we are — sequestered here in this university room in the labyrinth."

Nate sounded worried. After all, it was his student status which allowed the schemers to rent the space for purported business development. He remained steadfastly against the wall with knees to his chest and feet planted firmly on cold concrete.

Pumping his arms downward in a calming gesture, Kalen elaborated. "We owe you an explanation of what happened and intended to tell you at our next rendezvous ... which ended up being this frantic call to arms over the Ethos trial data. So first, it was Uncle Cy only. It was an unofficial questioning, but the interrogation took place at FSPA. I'm guessing to scare Cali and I into talking.

"They must have gotten wind of something we said. They thought Project Paint was the mastermind behind the defacing of *TuramaliScape* and the social riot. They believed we either started it or became a part of it. They had tracked our purchase of chalk and believed we initially intended to use chalk rather than paint. Kinda funny really ..."

"But how did they hear about Project Paint? We've been so careful." Nate pushed for more detail. "Spook. Do they know about Spook?"

"Spook. Uncle Cy hinted at the sophisticated firewall and not being able to track internet addresses. He suspects, but we gave no acknowledgement of using any sneaky technology." Kalen chuckled. "Nate, Zaner, you could probably get work at the federal agency someday if you wanted."

The schemers burst out laughing. Zane and Nate working side-by-side at FSPA was a comical concept. Finally, some humor to break the gravity of the discussion.

When laughter subsided, Kalen added a final note, still sidestepping the query about how Project Paint became known to Uncle Cy. "As far as this meeting location and fellow schemers … except for Cali and I, you're all safely anonymous. At least for now."

Wanting to jump in before the awkward question came up again about how anyone got wind of Project Paint, Cali picked up where her brother left off.

"Uncle Cy concluded that Kalen and I are involved in legit action which is a media campaign to undermine the EthosBot. No plan to destroy property, injure others, or do anything illegal. He simply requested we share the exposé that we compose about the clinical trials prior to posting. That way, he and his fellow agents can be prepared for social upheaval when the data is revealed. It seemed like a fair request."

"He promised we wouldn't be followed or surveilled either," Kalen added.

"After I spoke with Dr. Rane, my mom hinted at wanting to read the report from the interview. It's fair, guys. She may even have insight. Which is next on our docket for discussion … everything I learned from Dr. Rane. It builds on what Z and Kalen found with the clinical trial cases."

"Okay. Off the hook then," Zia determined with squinty eyes. "We're sharing our compositions with Uncle Cy and your mom before we go public. No fussing around too long waiting for their feedback though. We give them a timeframe for getting comments back to us and then we go public. And, we don't have to integrate their edits unless we as a team decide to do so." In a listen-to-me stubborn adamance, Z crossed her arms in front of her chest and rippled her toes against the concrete floor.

Zaner was the one to begin the ensuing round of laughter. He saluted his sister, "You got it."

"Cal, tell us what you uncovered in your meeting with Dr. Rane," Kalen prompted.

"Interviewing him was different than I imagined it would be. His history with this biotechnology dates to the beginning of turamali and bots. He's a psychiatrist with deep experience and brilliant insight. His honesty about the EthosBot surprised me.

"First, he took some time to explain how challenging mental and emotional health are to manage. Even in seemingly straightforward common afflictions such as anxiety and depression, individual nuances mean variations in what's effective for each person. Stressors, perceptions to stressors, and the corresponding moods or behaviors elicited are as unique as each person.

"As stated earlier, there was no specific crystal consistently associated with healing these conditions, and conversely, no demographic, physical, or mental characteristic per se that predicted what type of crystal would heal.

"We've seen what's been reported by *TIA*, and indeed the trials have yielded mixed results. Ethos has improved anxiety and depression for some while others not. From a clinical trial standpoint, he stated EthosBot is a statistical failure. It has not demonstrated efficacy by medical standards.

"He went on to say that Ethos does not meet medical safety standards either. The Earth event was one piece of evidence. Other evidence is that employees were sickened by exposure to what they assume was overwhelming crystal vibrational energy. No one understands the mechanism involved or why staff became ill. They simply changed processes, excused staff from the project, and shuffled things around to accommodate those unable to think clearly. Some employees were newly diagnosed with anxiety or depression just from working on the Ethos project. None of it made sense then nor makes sense now.

"Healing mental distress is actually quite fragile and nebulous. Finally, Dr. Rane called the use of Ethos reckless."

Kalen stretched forward on the bench with his elbows resting on his thighs. "Cal, Dr. Rane didn't mention changes in personality or belief systems? Nothing about what the trial volunteers described?"

"No, nothing. He was so candid as we talked. I wonder if he knew about the fundamental alterations in attitude, preferences, lifestyles ... sure seems like he would have told me."

"Do you think they even evaluated trial volunteers for those aspects? Then again, who would think to do so? Clinically, they were looking for improvement in symptoms related to anxiety and depression, not changes in religious or political affiliations, nor choice of recreational activity or nutrition." Kalen rubbed his hands repeatedly across his thighs. "Depression may make someone less active, lose or gain weight, not participate in social things, but conventional meds don't change your belief systems."

Kalen stood, touched his chin, and then waving his arm and pointing to the group continued speculating. "The researchers didn't look, ask, but we did. We thought to ask because ... although the physiology of crystal therapy on physical body or infectious ailments is based in biochemistry ... we still only hypothesize about the mechanics of crystals and the original virus on neurotransmitters and telepathy. Not truly understanding the phenomenon of telepathy while meddling further in synaptic machinations to undue mental illness led us to wonder about the effect on fundamental character. Guys, we asked, probed. They didn't."

"Whoa. This is so deep," Zane emphatically stated as he held his arms wide to depict the enormity of the situation. "If the trial researchers didn't discover character changes, and we go public with our data, it's gonna blow *TIA* out of the water. Their own people won't know what hit 'em."

Still slouched against the wall, Nate shook his head in agreement. He still required the cold solid concrete feel beneath him. He'd never witnessed nor been a part of such startling, perturbing evidence generation. He was a data guy, who thought he had already seen quite a bit of disturbing data for his youthful age.

"I should ask Dr. Rane," Cali offered. "I wonder if he knows anything about what the clinical trial cases told Z and Kalen."

Zia smirked, "We're smarter than the clinical trial experts. Gotta love it. We knew the little bot was devious long before they did, and now we can prove it."

The tryst & schemers laughed, bantered, and as usual, came up with their next step. Take the acquired information and write with a fury. They'd shuffle the narratives among themselves, then Uncle Cy and Sage. Without delay, they'd go public in only a matter of days.

It was getting late, and they all had class or places to be the next morning. Zane helped Nate off the floor, and Zia tucked into her sandals. Carson pushed off from his seated position, and Cali bolted toward the door.

As they were getting ready to leave, Zia voiced a notion that had been bothering her. "I wonder how Uncle Cy heard about Project Paint? I mean, which one of us would have said that in a place where he was around? Strange, right? Unless he picked up thought transference ... which doesn't make sense either, since we named the project the night the adults were all away at Jake and Kehlani's where he would have been distracted. After that, we've met here and used all forms of dialogue with high secrecy and shielding."

Zia looked around at everyone. Shoulders shrugged

and some rubbed chins.

Wanting to avoid further close contact, Cali was purposefully steps ahead of Carson. Now, she wanted to avoid the stare of her closest friend.

Carson was awkwardly ambulating toward the door when he paused midstride. "It was me," Carson confessed. "I thought I was protecting Cali. She was so upset about the sandstorm and injuries that I worried about what she might decide to do, and too, how others could hurt her. I thought Uncle Cy, being a federal agent, could keep an eye on her ... keep her safe. But my actions were misconstrued and obviously misguided. Sorry, I apologize to everyone. It's all on me."

The room went silent, until Zia simply said, "Carson."

"Truly sorry. I'll understand if you kick me out."

Carson continued shuffling out following Cali. As the room emptied, quiet hung heavily over the group. In the hallway, conversation became whispers and plans for heading home.

Unfortunately, Cali had come with Carson out of simple logistical convenience. They both resided at the hacienda. Kalen and Zia had been in a late class together, so they had traveled earlier in a single vehicle.

Cali paused for Carson to catch up to her at the top of the long concrete, spiral stairway. Carson approached Cali and gently guided her away from the top step and against the nearby wall. He had to do this now, because once at the hacienda, Cali would briskly head to the main casa. He placed both hands on her shoulders and looked into her eyes.

"Cal, I love you. I watch you move around the barn, ride ... and my heart beats faster. You're beautiful in every way. I want to be with you ... continue our relationship ...

what we had. But I'm not gonna beg to be loved by you. You have the right to choose. I want you to know that I'll wait for you to decide ... as long as it takes ... as many other guys you date. And, if I'm not the one in the end, just tell me straight up."

After opening his heart to Cali, Carson couldn't resist. He pulled her close into a bear hug caressing her entire body and kissing the top of her head. Then he slowly let her go.

Cali's eyes were moist as she tried to hold back the stream of tears just waiting to run down her face. "Carson ... I ... need to get home."

Kalen and Zia held back as they observed the interaction. Kalen was not worried about Carson, but then again, Cali was his twin, and he looked out for her. Too, Kalen felt Carson's pain. He would feel the same way if Zia — smart, silly, devious-bot-obsessed Z ever left him.

Beneath a clear, chilly, star-studded desert sky, the tryst & schemers made their way home.

Scheming done. At least for some, trysting didn't have a chance tonight.

Chapter 12

SANITY SEEKERS

Bot-teamers huddled in Turamali's Edge. Conversation was whispered but quite vehement. Deployment of the energy harmonizer to cause yet another disruptive solar-EMF Earth event had been an ongoing contentious topic over the past few weeks with this elite group of *Turamali Innovative Arts* employees.

Turamali's Edge was *the* place for staff to share work experiences in a safe and confidential manner. It was designed as a creative and restorative space for bot-teamers, with an open, welcoming, comfortable energy. Turamali's Edge was originally named the Creative Pod, but with the advent of the Radiance and Assault Bots, it was renamed. Over time, it was clear there was always a next precipice or edge to confront. Thus, interminably on the edge of Turamali.

"This is out of control. Fissures? More injuries? I did not sign up for this!" Several bot-teamers chimed in with similar sentiments.

"The first one was supposed to end Ethos. That tragedy was not enough? You had to channel another solar-EMF storm through the system?"

"You five ... you five bot-teamers are morphing into the very people you're trying to stop. They wield EthosBot over fundamental character, and you ... you theurgists wield geomagnetic solar storms over the Southwest and its creatures like a god!"

The five rogue engineers called themselves the theurgists — derived from Latin and Greek meaning divine workers or sorcerers — which indeed they believed they were. From their intellectual and innovative acumen sprung the energy harmonizer device which craftily wove solar, electromagnetic, and crystal energies into channeled mayhem. They deemed their work divine as it would stop Ethos.

Dissension over Ethos reigned in sharp contrast to the early years of BioBot development. At the outset, the project to alleviate anxiety and depressive disorders was the true engagement of bot-teamers' expertise in the sciences — genetics, neurobiology, crystallography, rheology, pharmacology, and more. The Technology, Biologics & Intelligent Life, and Crystal BioBot Teams absolutely thrived in their work. It was meaningful, purposeful, and outright fun working alongside professional peers who also loved their work.

Thus, the teams were enthusiastically motivated to develop the EthosBot1. As sure as there were multiple renditions of the Radiance and Assault Bots, there were bound to be next-gen bots to treat another emotional/mental health affliction. A long-term mission doing what they loved. It was pure joy.

As the Ethos clinical trials kicked off, outcomes were less than anticipated. However, that's science. That's medicine. Progress can be slow. Further, the team knew that tackling the human ethos was far different than tackling typical physical disease.

With each successive trial, though, the results became dicey and progressively frightening. Dicey as in sometimes the BioBot was successful, but too often, equally not. Frightening because trial volunteers spoke about changes in attitude and lifestyle. As they randomly conversed with their assigned *TIA* health practitioner, volunteers did so nonchalantly but still with an odd sentiment.

"Can't stand the taste of peanut butter anymore. Strange, I've eaten it my entire life as a protein source."

"Always voted for the global candidate. Now, I know that we need to focus on our nation alone. Switched political parties, and I think Ethos helped me figure that out."

"Can't bring myself to coach my little leaguers any longer. Too many people and kids around. Taking up yoga. Can you believe it? Traded noisy, energetic little ones and coaching for peaceful posing and stretching!"

The comments *may* have been noted in electronic volunteer patient records where *potentially* clinical practitioners read them and made the connection. Regardless, the comments were thoroughly assimilated into water cooler and Turamali Edge bot-teamer bantering. They chatted about the interesting comments and phenomena as soon as it began.

No one could define a day or week or even month when enthusiastic work turned controversial and hostile. It simply morphed and came into being. First, the overriding sentiment was dissatisfaction with patient results, as well as distrust of the integrity of the Ethos project and the leadership that allowed it to continue despite not reaching predetermined milestones.

Then, trial volunteer comments increasingly turned freaky, with not just changes in attitude and lifestyle, but regarding out-of-body experiences and moving between world portals. Staff became ill and a crusade formed among bot-teamers. With a righteous bent, they called themselves the sanity seekers.

The sanity seekers included some in leadership; albeit, some were merely silently observant, while others were in the thick of it, plotting equally despite having direct accountability to C-suite executives. Ouch. Definitely a risky ouch, as who knew who was legitimately committed to the clandestine effort versus spying to tow the company line?

Initially though, the sanity seekers respectfully followed the corporate chain of command with their concerns, but they felt dismissed, unheard, and not taken seriously by the decision makers. Thus, they felt they were stuck trying to figure out how to interrupt or stop the Ethos trials using their own ingenuity and wiles. Or perhaps, they could reveal to the world what they knew, and bend the power of the global audience to put the brakes on the madness.

Some vented through sympathetic friends and family who would hopefully shield the real source of intel in social posts. At the time social discourse began, *TIA* was hip deep in managing staff who became ill from working with the EthosBot, so they didn't give proper attention to rogue negative social posts. After all, the biotech company was familiar with negative media attention. They also knew sentiment undulated from positive to negative and back again under the influence of social whims.

Other bot-teamers indicated they were collecting data to share with a journalist or media person willing to listen. These individuals planned to terminate their employment when they had the data, and then go on the record as the verifiable source of intel on Ethos. They'd be respected for their bravery and gutsiness to takedown EthosBot. Surely, a rival biotech firm would hire them.

The theurgists, whip-smart engineers and crystallographers were sanity seekers who split from the dull group mindset. Ethos was increasingly out of control and the milquetoast sanity seeker maneuvers were feeble and futile. The theurgists brazenly conjured the Earth events, which to their delight stirred local protest, reckless social chatter, and world attention. *They* were the change agents.

With the blame quickly falling on the EthosBot for the geomagnetic storms, *TIA* would have to succumb to social and political pressures to end Ethos. Legitimate from a civil or employee standpoint or not, such was the thinking and intention of ... well, whip-smart employees who sincerely believed their undertaking was ethical and necessary to save people from the evils of Ethos.

Most sanity seekers supported the theurgists' first wild plan to time an upcoming, unusually large solar flare with the creation of an unforgettable Earth event. To be honest, seekers were experts from all walks of science, but none of them truly believed that a modest collection of solar cells hobbled together by the mad fivesome would capture the sun's rogue energy, synch with EMFs and crystals ... and then deliver an electrifying haboob with seismic activity, animal stampedes, and physical harm to life.

Did the sanity seekers believe an Earth event would garner attention? Attention, yes. Injury and fear, no. Or such was the initial general group belief. Still, water cooler conversation and heated debate was never-ending. Should they, or shouldn't they experiment with their homegrown science project to make an activist statement?

In the end, there were those who took social action, while others chose to support and chat on, risking nothing. At the proper meteorological time, the theurgists took it upon themselves to operationalize their concocted engineering wonder, the energy harmonizer.

The first Earth event was timed by the theurgists to coincide with a significant solar wind shock wave. Within hours of event mayhem, the Federal Security and Pursuit Agency was at the front entrance of *TIA* meeting with corporate executives, security teams, and Team Leads. The warrant was swift, but honestly, the C-suite execs had become so familiar working with the FSPA that a warrant didn't matter.

Since the original unsanctioned eco-bot launch, the federal agency had become an instrumental partner in thwarting industrial espionage and theft of the biotechnology. Domestic and global biotech competitors sought it, as well as nations desiring to heal or bend the human ethos.

Agent Cyprus Desai and his team searched for the culprits involved in the Earth events. They knew there was a seed of discontent that originated within *Turamali Innovative Arts*. Or at the very least, there was a distinct thread of rebellion that wove through *TIA* connecting to mainstream social activists.

After the first solar-electromagnetic storm, federal agents had gotten nowhere with employees. It appeared that many were disgruntled and said very little when questioned. A few admitted there were diverse groups among staff who were actively pursuing ways to stop the use of the EthosBot. However, no one was willing to point fingers or give the FSPA any breadcrumbs to follow.

Too, insider telepathic conversations were heavily cloaked. Bot-teamers weren't only Hyperintelligent and Insightful, many were Adept. Agent Desai and his team were stymied.

The second Earth event obviously pushed many

bot-teamers to rethink their role in anti-Ethos activities, and their quiet support of others who were clearly causing tragedy. Surely having knowledge of the energy harmonizer and its purpose, and not telling any authority — internal or external to *TIA* — implied some measure of guilt for the sympathetic but quiet bot-teamers.

Alternatively, innocent social posting revealing insider intel should be on a different scale of justice — or such was believed by employees attempting to reconcile their conscience. After all, violating company confidentiality agreements to tell the world about the reality of EthosBot treatment was different than jerry-rigging a device to create freaky neurobiologically disruptive storms that left animals running for their lives and humans cowering.

External scrutiny by the FSPA intimidated *Turamali Innovative Arts* employees compelling them to reconceive the Ethos situation. Telepathic conversations teemed with controversy, agitation, and fear.

What is our responsibility or liability in word-fomented mayhem versus physical catastrophe? ... Is the scale of crime different? ... Do different ends justify if the action was indeed righteous? ...

The theurgists are criminals. They caused real harm. In contrast, the word-weavers are simply activists inspiring debate and peaceful protest.

One notion was clear among sanity seekers. They were furious with the theurgists. Earth crevasses and more pain were not condoned by the majority of anti-Ethos bot-teamers. So, for several more minutes, the infamous fivesome, divine sorcerers were lambasted.

"Where is this solar array, this energy harmonizer? It must be located here at *TIA* or somewhere near *TuramaliScape*. The rest of us have agreed this needs to stop. We're dismantling your device, or we're gonna watch you do it."

The five transgressors smirked and avoided a response. They liked the feeling of having control. Finally, one of the engineers spoke up.

"We have done harm. Unintentional, but nonetheless, we sadly acknowledge the tragic injuries. However, we're the ones so far stirring up worldwide debate over the legitimate use of Ethos. Your social postings are the same old chit-chatter. We, however, have made people stop and think about the crystal power of EthosBot. We, the technocrats, made them feel it … that is neurobiologically for you Intelligent Life teamers. We also made them see it, all around them."

Empowered by the most pretentious of the theurgists, another piped up with her own proclamation.

"We may have caused some tragedy, but if we had not forced the issue and capitalized on the harnessing of this type of energy, millions more would suffer if Ethos became mainstream medicine. How does a society go on when millions if not billions succumb to EthosBot, rather than simply being who they are, or who they freely choose to be without the influence of a bot?"

The equally emboldened angry bot-teamers persisted, "Where? Where is your device? We need to know, or you show us where it's located."

Smirking and deciding it possibly was not a big deal to share some detail, the pretentious theurgist leader declared, "Of course, it's in the desert. The device itself is not in *TIA's* basement as some have speculated. It's a super-specialized collector to capture solar and electromagnetic energy, functioning much like a signal is to a satellite. We could take you there or provide coordinates. Or you can see the entire setup on our private virtual network in the bowels of …"

He purposefully trailed off not wanting to reveal more.

The sanity seekers determined to destroy the energy harmonizer were cut short on their immediate objective. A small group of like-minded bot-teamers came rushing into Turamali's Edge.

With alarm and vehemence, they barged right into the heated dialogue with each relaying a snippet of news.

"Exposé! Someone's posted our clinical trial data! It's crazy too. Sophisticated predictor variable models and anonymous quotes from trial volunteers. The stuff is legit."

"They know. The world knows now. They know Ethos changes people. Fundamentally. Religiously, politically, socially, the very essence of who they are and how they choose."

"It's someone with the cyber alias, TripleTempest. So, maybe it's three people involved, but one brazen enough to research and write the unvarnished truth ... Who could it be?"

"They even interviewed one of our psych consults. Not sure which one, but if we analyze the report, we might be able to guess who this TripleTempest got to. It's more evidence. It backs up everything the trial volunteers told this Tempest person. Or Tempest trio."

"We're already trying to trace the internet protocol address, but I'm guessing if they're smart enough to get this intel, they're smart enough to hide behind a firewall and a series of misdirected digital footprints."

"Guys, people! This is it. It's gonna tip the C-suite to stop Ethos."

With the sudden announcement of a pivotal exposé, the Edge turned strangely quiet. Formerly unheard over the commotion of speech-making, serene music filtered throughout the space. Water curtains burbled over stone walls. Awareness was reset.

After a minute, the most vocal bot-teamer ready to destroy the solar storm generating device whispered. "Are we done then? We wait to see what happens tomorrow? By then, nations will have made their media pronouncements, and the C-suite will surely respond to all of this by making a formal statement to pause or end Ethos. If the exposé is as true as you describe, this company has much to acknowledge and atone."

The sanity seekers, theurgists included, agreed to pause further action and regroup tomorrow. Methodically, they took their beverages in tow returning to their workstations in the Art Studio. The turn of events left most agitated, whispering in pairs, and wondering what would happen if Ethos production was truly shut down. The very event they wanted to occur, now seemed too real. Surely, it would impact their daily work and potentially their job at *TIA*.

Yet, there remained the emboldened few who quietly signaled among themselves the intention to meet late in the afternoon in the subterranean room. The theurgists had alluded jokingly to the energy harmonizer itself not being located there, but perhaps their control operation was indeed sublevel — in a remote location of *TIA* most employees had never seen nor were allowed access.

Truer things are said in prideful jest. This was one jest some of the bot-teamers angriest over human and animal injury were heck-bent to follow up on. Once you're on a mission, it's hard to let go or wait for C-suite executives or world pressure to force responsible action.

No more cries from Coyote or Cougar … or the herds of horses. No more human catastrophe from a machine built to create weird haboobs with incapacitating electromagnetic fields and holes in Mother Earth. We end this.

Thus, the courageous and infuriated telepathed among themselves and to receptive allies on the outside responsible for the exposé.

Chapter 13

ENDING ETHOS

Did you hear? That urgent telepathed message? Clearly sent by someone with enough skill to reach us. TripleTempest. It's meant for us. Although not with Kalen or Zia as she jogged across the *TuramaliScape* campus, Cali thought transferred to them as she strode from one class to another.

Urgent and clear, Kalen replied. *Someone from inside BioBot land is going to destroy whatever it is that set off the geostorms ... an energy harmonizer?*

Wow, huge wow, Zia chimed in. *Now, we know there's a device involved for certain. Those sympathetic insiders turned activist before we did. Too, they reached out to TripleTempest. Finally, telepathed us. What the heck took them so long? We need to tell Zane and Nate. Cal, include Carson too?*

Cali hesitated, but something deep inside compelled her to telepath a definitive reply. *Yeah, feels like we should. Perhaps some role Carson has yet to play. Not sure, but instinct tells me we spread the word with all the tryst & schemers. Something's brewing, guys. Our TripleTempest exposé has triggered action. Could be a long night.*

Gabe, Cali pondered. I should share some of this with him. Weird I feel this way, but if something is stirring … conspiring and rogue action … having a medic or another person in-the-know could be helpful. Huh. Helpful or may outright save us. Carson and Gabe. I *am* a mess. Am I bringing them both into this new tangle of intel because it's the right thing to do, or because I'm unconsciously a plotting drama princess? Save me. Someone, freakin' save me, as Zia would say.

Suddenly, communication devices buzzed with a news update.

'Upon urgent recommendation from our medical consultants, *Turamali Innovative Arts* is immediately suspending use of the EthosBot. Trial volunteers with the embedded bot are requested to contact their dedicated *TIA* healthcare professional. Individual assessments will be made promptly regarding BioBot retention or removal. Related research, development, and production of the EthosBot will also be suspended.'

Pain point hit. Our exposé turned the tide. Kalen wanted to shout exuberantly from a team effort well done.

Zia, Zane, and Nate sent their own exclamatory telepathic messages to their fellow schemers as well. Even Carson congratulated the group.

Gabe telepathed Cali with equal applause. *Cali, I can only imagine that Sage Amaris' daughter had a role in TIA suspending Ethos. Based on your insider info, if the storm device is going to be destroyed or accidently activated again, we need to be ready. Cal, tell that agent uncle of yours.*

Gabe, I want to … see you. Soon. Cali stammered in her telepathic transference.

Gabe gave no reply. Perhaps, he was caught up in a

work rescue. Maybe, he had to consider. Regardless, Cali felt suddenly empty.

Breaking the spell she was under in a Gabe moment, her brother messaged her. *Cal, we should get with Uncle Cy. Right away. Like now, even if we're late for next class.*

Kalen and Cali found a secluded place on campus to make contact. In the moment, Cyprus felt obligated to let the message go to voicemail. His team was following Indra Sukarno, a former international criminal who was now traipsing the perimeter of *T-Scape*.

When Uncle Cy didn't pick up their call, the twins telepathed him with urgency. *We know about the device that generated the geomagnetic storms. Called the energy harmonizer. Something is happening. Tonight. At TIA.*

Despite getting awfully close to several suspects inside the biotech company and even the originating geographic location of the storms, the FSPA had not identified the culprits nor the device. The last message from the twins startled him. Agent Cyprus Desai held up his hands in a stop-wait signal to his team. He called his teens.

After the call with Uncle Cy, Kalen spoke privately with his sister. "Cali, I've never heard Uncle Cy so tense. He sounded as if he was working a covert operation while we conversed. I got the distinct feeling that what we just learned from *TIA* insiders is related to his op and his edict for us to leave campus right away."

"Agree. Our intel about a move to destroy the energy harmonizer seemed to give him pause, but also elevated the intensity of how he spoke."

Trying to sort out the situation, Kalen stared intently across the acreage at the formidable biotech company. With hands resting on hips, he barely breathed before reiterating what they knew, hoping the quick turn of events would soon make sense.

"He stated they're closing campus mid-afternoon due to a power grid matter. We should be receiving a directive shortly meant for all university and business personnel to exit campus promptly. Those in residence will be advised to remain inside. So, Nate can stay put, but we need to leave? ... Power grid matter must be a ruse to get people away."

Just then, their phones chimed with the predicted message to all staff and students. Cali shook her head in disbelief wondering if their single conversation with Uncle Cy precipitated a shuttering of college and business buildings ... or had something else already been in motion?

"It's as if the FSPA is aware something is stirring over at *TIA,* and our info added to the dilemma." Cali pulled a hair tie from her pack and finger-brushed her hair into a quick ponytail. "We've got work to do."

"Cal, no. Uncle Cy was adamant we leave campus as soon as we receive the directive. He even added that we should not be alarmed, nor suspicious as is our nature. He wants us at the hacienda well before sunset. Cali, the feds are tracking someone or a group. You can bet on it. If that's indeed true, then we should not intervene or be around here."

"But who the heck is he tracking? It bugs me." Cali gently kicked at the park bench in frustration. "I'll acquiesce to his edict, but I want mom departing with us. Zia, Zaner, and Nate too. Nate's just gonna have to leave his dorm and come with us. If something is transpiring that's got Uncle Cy alarmed, we need mom and our fellow schemers with us."

They agreed to pull their fellow schemers and mother together for an urgent meetup at this very park bench on campus. Together as a group, they'd all head to the hacienda. From there, Zia and Zane could go home, and Nate could remain at the casa for as long as needed — at least until the day's happenings were sorted out.

The twins felt a sense of foreboding. It seemed to get heavier with every passing minute as they waited for their fellow schemers.

Nate was the last tryst & schemer to join the group in the open green space on campus. Agent Uncle Cy's role in this strange situation overruled the college's simple advisory to remain inside the dormitory, and so Nate joined his friends arriving fully prepared. He had two backpacks — likely his bug out bag and no doubt his slew of electronic devices. Nate barely greeted his companions when Cali turned unusually serious.

"Mom's missing. Not replied to me. You?" Cali asked Kalen.

"Weird. I assumed she'd be the last one here with work and all, but silence from mom. No text, nor telepathic communication."

"Let's head to *TIA*. It's right over there. Just go through visitor access and find her. Right?" Zia was anxious to get the final wayward member of the group and speed away from *T-Scape*. Like the others, she was feeling increasingly edgy.

Cali acknowledged Zia, and then studied her brother before addressing him. "I'll go. I'll go find mom. You go with the group to the hacienda. Get outta here before any doom." Attempting to be in control and lighten the moment, she smiled sideways.

"No," Kalen was adamant. "Cali, we hit the company's pain point today, and they made the announcement we've been trying to eke out of them for months. Then suddenly the storm generating device has a name and is being discussed by insiders determined to destroy it. The exposé hit a nerve, started an avalanche. Too much risk. You are not going to *TIA* alone to look for mom. Especially since she seems to be MIA, missing in action."

Now, Zia was trembling and biting her lip, but her demeanor screamed defiance. "We're staying put and helping, and it's not negotiable! If the proverbial you-know-what is gonna hit the fan, then we're your backups."

As she spoke, her resolve hardened and her bravery fortified. "We'll figure out how to spread across campus and watch you. Watch the building. Watch the area. I'm near Adept status and will work with you and others around the building telepathically. Cal, Kalen, you're not alone." Only in Z fashion could it be stated in such a manner.

The group was so involved in serious dialogue, they were surprised when Carson strode toward them. Now, the tryst & schemers were whole.

"Hey," Carson greeted his fellow schemers somewhat timidly. "Bayani and Uncle Cy told me you'd be heading to the hacienda in haste, and I was to look out for your arrival and the ranch with heightened senses. When you didn't show up when Cyprus said you would, I figured I better come here and find you. I feel it too. It's in the air, an eerie vibration. Something wicked is imminent."

Without overthinking, Cali gave Carson a quick greeting hug, then squeezed both his forearms looking straight at him. "Kalen and I are getting inside *TIA* now to find my mother and get her out. Work with the group. Zia's forming a reconnaissance around the exterior of the building and will intercept and relay messages as she receives them. Have to assume something funky is goin' on."

Without waiting for anyone's reply, Cali grabbed her brother's arm. Together they lightly jogged to the concrete fortress about a half mile away.

♦

As Sage finally escaped work for the day and walked briskly toward the meetup with her teens, she was taken aback by premonition. A woman in dark harem pants with a breezy ivory tunic and Panama hat approached Sage.

She looks familiar. I know her, Sage thought to herself.

In a swift motion, the woman adeptly grabbed Sage's arm and swung her with expert dexterity into retracing the steps back to her place of employment. The woman kept her arm linked with Sage's and pulled her inward whispering in her ear like an old friend.

"Say nothing or you know how quick I can be to silence the uncooperative."

"Indra. My god. Indra Sukarno. What ... what's happening? I thought you were on our side now. Working with Agent Desai over the past years."

Sage paused in midstride and turned to study Indra's face. Indra seemed fine with the pause as it manifested the ruse of old friends unexpectedly running into one another.

"Sage, the less you know, the better. I ask you to trust me." Sukarno removed her sunglasses and raised an eyebrow as she stared at her old nemesis. To Indra, Sage had weathered the years with grace, but there was a toll that showed deep beneath the graying hair and now slimmer, fragile physique.

Raising teens or your work at TIA? Indra telepathed not anticipating a reply.

"Now here's what's going to happen. You're going to give us access to your workspace. You forgot something, or you want to show an old friend the charming, news-worthy biotech research firm. Although, if my source is correct, security should not be a problem. We're headed to the subterranean level."

"Indra, I could try to fight you off. Create a scene. But I don't want to. I don't have the energy and you know it." They picked up their forward advance to *TIA*.

"My dear Sage." Sukarno laughed as if to display that the two were sharing memorable humor. "If you must know, Agent Desai and his amigos — as you say in the Southwest — are nearby. Play this out with me. You're smart enough to do this." Indra picked up Sage's nearest hand and gave it a squeeze as if to seal the deal.

"Indra. You better be wearing the white hat today. I need to telepath my kids. They're ..."

"No. Don't open the discussion with them. Keep them safe."

Interestingly, that was the first statement from Indra that Sage believed without question. Whatever is happening, best keep my kids out of this. They better not be hanging around here after the advisories.

Evening shadows grew long, and a chilly breeze rolled in from the north. Cali and Kalen suddenly froze in place. Perhaps forty or fifty yards away, it appeared their mother was arm in arm with someone wearing a flouncy hat and walking back toward *TIA*.

Kalen immediately telepathed Uncle Cy.

The return message was more than forceful. It was angry, unlike any message Kalen had received from his uncle.

Kalen, Cali, stand down. Go back to your friends. I'm nearby. Now. Go. Go back with Carson to the hacienda. Now, kids, now.

Cali trembled, and unaware, tears of fear ran down her cheeks. "Kalen, we follow mom. We've got to."

"With you, Cali Cal. So, so ... very with you on this one."

With that, the twins jogged up behind their mother and Flouncy Hat, just as they had gained building access. Placing a hand on the entwined pair's shoulders in a broad embrace, Kalen leaned between his mother and Flouncy Hat, "You're not leaving us behind." Kalen continued to feign escorting the pair through the doorway in a jovial manner.

Sage perceptibly stiffened. Still entwining Sage's arm, Indra simply turned in feigned surprise toward Cali and Kalen. "Oh, how wonderful. Family's in on it. I suggest you head home though. The hacienda is it still? There's a storm coming, I hear."

Indra paused a beat before continuing the charade. "Your mom and I go way back. We won't be long." Indra stared meaningfully at the twins hoping to relay a message that would frighten them into departing the building. They were not part of the plan. *Your Uncle Cy, Agent Desai awaits you.*

The teens were fully unnerved now. Flouncy Hat knows our mom, Uncle Cy, and the hacienda.

Cali telepathed Kalen. *That story that mom told us as kids. The spy called Indra Sukarno. Is this her? Maybe it wasn't a story.*

Then, Cali observed the jewel, the yellow sapphire embedded in a sleek band across the apparent spy's forehead. Harem pants, the anklet, hand-embroidered ballet flats fit for a double-oh-seven secret agent woman and any required acrobatics. *You're Indra Sukarno.*

Shrugging her shoulders, Indra simply truncated the exchange. She did not want Sage's teenagers involved. They're so unpredictable. "We'll see you later." The pair walked past an expansive rain curtain to the grand staircase where they proceeded to the lowest level of *TIA*.

The teens looked around the grand foyer. *Where's se-*

curity? Is this part of Uncle Cy's plan?

Then, they both heard Zia. *Cal, Kalen, three darkly clad culprits are entering the security tunnel. The one we're not supposed to know about. Watch your backs.*

Enough already. In spooky twin agreement, they followed their mother and the storied spy down … down.

♦

Agent Desai watched as his teens defied his command. Not much disturbed the highly trained professional. He was known for his unflappable character. Paired with his intellect and skills, Agent Desai was agent extraordinaire. Except, obviously, when it came to his Cali and Kalen. He slammed his night visions on the ground and grabbed his head with both hands stomping as he paced.

"Sir, we've got the building surrounded. It seems their friends are surrounding the *TIA* building too. Do you want us to pick them up? We can make sure they come quietly."

Cyprus considered his strategy. His operatives knew how to quickly and quietly immobilize with swift pressure to the right physiologic point. That would get the others safely out of the way of the operation.

Cy spoke in a low tone. "We don't know what's going to transpire tonight. Get these teenagers out. Should be at least three of them — Zia, Zane, and Nate. Carson, too, maybe if joined their hare-brained reconnaissance. Bring them back here. Set up a tent. Make them comfortable until they become conscious. We may need to secure their hands. They tend to be crafty. I want two agents stationed at the tent to keep these kids at bay." Agent Desai said plenty. Likely more than his teammates needed. They knew their job.

The squad's tactical earpieces buzzed with an update.

The three foreign mercenaries had infiltrated the building exactly as their intel had told the FSPA they would. They entered a little-known tunnel accessed by a metal ground plate hidden beneath prickly desert brush.

The tunnel had been part of the original architectural plan so that executives or security personnel could find a way out or into the concrete monolith, home to highly coveted secrets of the biotech company. One never knows when it could be time to run and hide. Or something even altogether different. Regardless, it was all about unmitigated access in any conceivable circumstance.

At the end of the tunnel, there was a heavy metal door, access-friendly only to those with the correct biometric. A biometric cleverly secured by Sukarno would give the foreign criminals access to the EthosBot and any other high-tech bot the culprits desired.

International crime made the planet so small these days, Indra thought. Feels like child's play. Oh wait, it is. Only, these are teens and young adults who believe they are the world's masterminds of engineering and biotechnology … hhhmmm … not tonight.

Sukarno arrived in the subterranean room with Sage still in tow. This was the location they believed served as the base for controlling the storm generating device. It was also believed to be the finest storehouse of BioBots.

She nudged Sage toward the biometric pad. It was a novel venous detection system, supposedly the best of the biometric authentication systems. The structure and pathways of veins on the underside of the arm were quite unique, and unlike fingerprints and even iris scans, were not generally subject to risks of trauma or biologic degradation.

Sage obliged and the door clicked open. Three people clad head to toe in dark armor pushed past Sage and Indra.

They held relatively small firearms and likely other hidden weapons. No matter, this invasion was considered a soft entry for them. They had an easy in, and no one would stop them. Everything they sought was housed right here at subterranean level.

Their mission was to locate the storm generating device and EthosBot, along with other BioBot samples and prototypes. Then, take the device and whatever bots they could get their hands on and depart. Stealthily positioned in open desert was an aircraft, their getaway — a getaway ideally only an hour away from mission accomplishment.

Sukarno was a good card but merely an implement to get the international criminals this far. They'd finish her off soon enough and fly to a remote locale. Or maybe, they'd just leave her behind, and she could fend for herself. If she survived FSPA, she might be useful in the future. No bridge burned as they say.

Sage led the way down a hallway to the wine cellar. Technically, it was the BioBot cellar, but teasingly, endearingly, authorized bot-teamers and C-suite execs referred to it as the wine cellar. It threw off most of the nefarious. Too, wine cellar sounded better than a cellar of BioBots. Happiness-creating wine sounded much better than bio-altering energized crystal bots. Wine cellar it was.

Surprisingly, the heavy doors to the cellar were ajar. The first door was another constructed of heavy metal, while the second door was constructed of thick sturdy wood. Sage paused as she heard voices.

Indra signaled to the three commandos to wait. She needed to assess the situation with Sage at her side. Together, they crept into the cellar.

Several employees were seated or standing around a large semi-circular table. Virtual screens were alive with images and calculations. Perceiving footfalls, two turned and gasped at the sight of Sage and Indra. Playing into the charade, Indra shoved Sage forward toward the group of about a dozen bot-teamers.

Sage stumbled, regained balance, and addressed the group. “What are you doing down here? The cellar is highly secured space.”

The theurgist leader stepped forward peering at Sage. “Who’s with you? What are *you* doing here? And with an outside friend, I might add.” He had no sooner gotten the words out with bravado, when he realized the situation was not simply other well-intentioned employees spying on the ill-intentioned. His swagger turned to stone and his face paled.

Sage stared at the countenances of the rogue employees and shook her head in a negative motion. Hesitantly, Sage spoke. “These thieves intend to take every BioBot sample stored in the cellar. Then, they want your storm generating device. I suggest we give it to them.”

This time, it was another brave soul who spoke, one of the irate sanity seekers. “We came down here to destroy the device, but it’s not here. And the BioBots are worthless in their current state. They’re not activated.”

Smart response, Sage thought, but is it enough to dissuade whatever Sukarno and the thieves have planned?

One of three black-clad thugs pulled his small firearm forward and slowly began toying with it. Another pulled a small but nonetheless lethal looking knife from a side leg pocket. Their stances widened.

The woman in dark harem pants tossed her hat aside onto the floor. Nudging Sage as if she was an object in her path, she slowly stepped in front of the two bot-teamers brave enough to challenge. Trying to intimidate, she whispered as she passed each one.

"My men are restless. We do not wish to use force." *Play along. I'm on your side.* "Tell us where the device is. It's imperative we take that if nothing else." *Telepath me and Sage. The men won't hear. Sage and I have an impenetrable shield around them.*

Indra was careful to take her time. She wanted her words to sink in, and the frightened bot-teamers would surely need time to figure out their next move.

"The device is in the desert. It's positioned there to collect solar flares and electromagnetic fields. You won't see it, though. It's concealed. We need ... we'd need to take you there." One of the theurgists believed providing true information that diverted them out of the subterranean chamber could only be advantageous.

This gets us out of here, right? You can help us escape then? Now humbled, the engineer assumed being in the open desert at night would provide better opportunity to end this ordeal.

"Enough dancing with these children," one of the thieves spoke with a thick accent, enunciating as if he was still learning the language. "Gentlemen, start loading up the BioBots. One of every type. Radiance1 to Radiance8. Assault1 et-cet-er-ah. Ethos. Many Ethos." The vocal mercenary was apparently thug captain.

The other two culprits in crime unhooked their bags, pulling out sophisticated containers and thin insulated gloves to handle the bots. They positioned themselves at opposite ends along the wall of cryogenic storage units. Obviously, they'd methodically work their way toward one another until all sample bots were collected.

Indra, Sage pleaded telepathically, *we can't let them take the bots, especially Ethos. And not the storm generator.*

They're too powerful. For anyone or any nation to wield. You must know that.

We destroy it all now. Right now. Tonight. The infuriated and insistent sanity seeker joined the telepathic conversation. *Ethos and this energy harmonizer will be catastrophic in the wrong hands.*

Sage felt her legs weaken beneath her, and she stumbled forward to a kneeling position. Indra raised her foot and nudged Sage in her back with her ninja-worthy ballet flat. "Get up. Show your comrades what you're made of." She continued the ploy and angled a look at the vocal thug, trying to assess his next move.

"Copy. Second and third forces in place." The thug captain spoke into his earbud.

Indra whirled around and stared at him. "Other forces? When did the plan change?"

He laughed, "Sukarno. You think we trust you? Mostly, but not one hundred as they say. Besides, this op too important without a lot of backup."

"We're collecting now. Yes, avoid contact with federal agents. Boss said no international fallout." He checked the time on his wrist device, and then looked up to assess how quickly his fellow mercenaries were making their way along the wall of bots. "Look for us in fifteen. Getting GPS coordinates for storm device."

Cy, Cy, they've got you surrounded. Other forces onsite. Talk to me! Sage was slow to rise keeping her head dropped so she could telepath and avoid eye contact.

In anger, she fisted a hand on the hard floor. *Why is telepathy stymied? I don't even hear the teens, and I know they're out there.*

Mom, Kalen and I are here. Behind the double doors ... listening. Afraid to telepath in case Sukarno picks up messaging. Seems she's on our side. Dear Higher Powers, I sure as heck hope so.

Upon hearing her daughter, Sage stifled a gasp and lifted her fist to her lips. *My kids. In thick of it.* To channel the supreme fear of having her children's lives in mortal jeopardy just feet away from her, she bit down hard on the index finger of her fisted hand.

The thug captain sauntered toward the bot-teamer who stated the device was in the desert. "GPS coordinates please." He held the cold steel of his modest firearm against the engineer's cheek, slowly rolling it down around his throat and back up to his forehead. "Don't be hero. Heroes die you know."

Knowing the good guys were surrounded — or so that appeared to be the situation on the outside — and hearing Sage's desperate plea, the defacto leader of the theurgists telepathed in earnest to everyone in the cellar except the black-clad thugs.

Give him the coordinates. Now. The screens here ... this is the control room for the energy harmonizer. We'll set the device to blow the cellar. That takes out Ethos, the other BioBots, and the entire device control center. They'll never get to the solar-EMF array in the desert. It will self-destruct in the process. I can set it for just that.

The savvy engineer never believed he'd be agreeing with the sanity seeker heck-bent on the destruction of his brainchild technology. The theurgists can build it better next time, he thought. And BioBot biologics are mainstream medicine. It'll all be back soon enough.

Not thinking her message of destruction meant simultaneous personal demise, the courageous sanity seeker shouted her telepathic message, *We die? We all die in the process too? Your idea of destruction means blowing up the cellar as we stand here?*

The bot-teamer with cold steel against his face stalled, listening intently to all thought transference. "Uh, okay. Let me think ..." He blinked, still avoiding, trying hard to listen to the silent dialogue in the room.

No, we don't die, the lead theurgist continued to telepath. *The ground beneath will begin to roll. Then we run while the thugs are figuring out what's happening. We all get out before the entire section of this building caves.*

We'll help get you out. We came down the grand staircase. It's the fastest way to ground level. Let the thugs get stuck with the tunnel exit. Kalen thought transferred.

Distraction, Kalen, Cali continued the open telepathic communication among the bot-teamers and Sukarno. *We've been working on telekinesis. We toss bots on the floor at the moment the device is set. Crashing bots and rolling ground will distract the criminals long enough for the rest of us to scramble out.*

To say the bot-teamers and Indra were keeping up and on board with the plan would be fantastical. Senses were heightened, and irrespective of consensus, the hasty plan appeared to be set.

Basically, the engineers believed the best strategy was to blow it all up to avoid theft, and certain future wielding of their and *TIA's* technology by the nefarious. Furthermore, in James Bond fashion, at least a few of the bot-teamers believed they'd make it out safely, while the cellar and part of the building disintegrated behind them, putting the evil-doers to permanent rest.

"Wait!" The defacto theurgist leader suddenly realized he'd need a reason to input the directive to the storm generator. They'd never let him start tapping screens for no apparent reason. "The coordinates. They're complicated.

We've moved the device several times already to protect it. Let me bring up the alphanumeric sequence."

The two thieves collecting bots turned and glanced at the group to be sure nothing unplanned was taking place. Pleased with everyone's attention on their mercenary pal, they continued their methodical work.

Pulling the firearm back toward his belt, the thug captain moved adjacent to the engineer. He watched as several screens were engaged at once. The captain had no idea what the lightning-quick icon tapping meant, but he observed anyway.

"So much work, tapping this, that ... to get me coordinates?"

Defying nerves, the theurgist guru played his role to the hilt. He simply tilted his head and raised an eyebrow as he appraised the ignorant thug. "I'm getting what you ask for." *And so much more.*

Indra realized this was her moment. She silenced one of her earpieces, and turning toward the back wall, she engaged another. Furtively, she whispered. "Cy, forces surround you. Check your back. Cali, Kalen here but hiding. Several bot-teamers were already in cellar. Engineer to engage storm device. Cellar building to explode. Get ready. Minutes away. Do you copy?"

Not believing what he heard, Cyprus leaned one of his hands heavily on the trunk of a mesquite tree. "Repeat."

"Check your back for other forces. Storm device being engaged. Cellar to explode. Look for us running."

"Copy. Oh my god, copy." Agent Desai was fairly certain he'd never said 'oh my god, copy' in his entire career. The other militant forces had been tracked, but an explosion with bot-teamers and his operative inside?

His second in command heard the transmission and

sent word to the field team.

In the subterranean recess of *TIA,* Cali and Kalen each caressed their Kehlani-gifted tourmaline amulet and focused their psychic energy on spilling BioBots onto the cellar floor. Thirty seconds passed. Nothing. Then, jolted by the sharp clatter of bot vials onto concrete, their eyes widened. Within seconds, the floor began to roll, and they instinctively grabbed each other's arm.

Barely audible in the mayhem, Kalen murmured to his sister, "Now is our time to run. Lead and run."

The sharp cracking sound of stray gunshots was interspersed with shouts in an unknown language. Kalen and Cali rushed in to escort the bot-teamers out and up the stairway. Sukarno already had her arm around Sage and was pushing her forward.

For Agent Desai and his team, barely a minute passed, and the ground rolled. The concrete structure remained solid. Then came loud cracking and crunching sounds with rolling that vibrated through their feet.

The energy harmonizer was a unique engineering wonder. Although no solar flare was tapped tonight, there was stored solar energy in the cells. Combined with amplification of the local electromagnetic fields and cryogenic crystal energy, the energy harmonizer device created the progressive explosion that ended it all.

Over nearly two minutes, the explosive wave grew. With the initial ground roll, the bot-teamers and Sukarno raced for their lives ... past the massive wood and metal doors through the hallway up the grand staircase and out the now shattered floor-to-ceiling windows in the *TIA* foyer. They had barely passed the building's entrance when concrete imploded and crushing chunks were blown hither and thither.

The massive cache of BioBots was destroyed. Geodes and crystals were strewn like shiny pebbles for miles around campus. Both components of the energy harmonizer only existed in the minds of the engineers — theurgists, divine sorcerers who fabricated it. Its physical manifestation no more.

Turamali Innovative Arts appeared broken in a sea of sand and crumpled palo verde, mesquite, pinyon pine, and desert brush.

Coyote and *Cougar* surveyed the terrain from afar. Justice.

Chapter 14

SECOND CHANCES

Having commandeered the rogue bot-teamers to escape from the cellar, Sukarno was the last to depart the building. Mission accomplished she thought, as she ran toward operatives anxious to escort the brave and bedraggled to safety. Dark sky friendly campus lighting revealed the line of Float vehicles and agents in the near distance.

Sage turned to wait for her former nemesis. At the surprise meetup, Sage wasn't at all sure if she could trust Indra or the situation she was being led into. Yet, Sukarno had pulled off the international ploy with her usual finesse. The outright destruction of the main supply of BioBots and the energy harmonizer was likely not part of the plan, but Sage felt abruptly and completely free now.

The oddly generated wind from the blast undulated Indra's torn harem pants against her legs as she lightly jogged across the terrain. Amusingly, she held her Panama hat in one hand. She'd saved the bot-teamers and her hat. What a story. Indra wryly smiled at Sage as she narrowed the distance between them.

Without warning, seismic activity rolled again sending

an additional barrage of concrete shrapnel into the air. Sage screamed at Indra throwing her arms to the side indicating to run sideways. The alert came too late. Indra Sukarno was hit in the back of her head, and she fell.

Still yelling "Sukarno", Sage slumped to Indra's side. She rolled her fellow comrade in crime over on her back, but Indra was limp and nearly lifeless.

"Indra, don't leave us," Sage implored. She grabbed Indra's hand bending forward listening to the barely audible coming from parched lips.

"Foe to ally … Sage … take … take sapphire … more on other side of portal for me … see you, see you, my … other side of veil …"

Indra Sukarno was gone. Sage remained motionless weeping with abandon, as she drifted back in time when Indra walked right onto the hacienda property with *Coyote* signaling events to come in the dark of night. Sage had been the eco-terrorist launching the botanical bot, while Indra had been the foreign operative sent by her Asian consortium to take bot-teamers and Adepts by force, if necessary, to heal what turamali wrought in the early days. So long ago, and yet not.

Swiftly kneeling next to Sage, Agent Desai wrapped his arm around her. He nodded to the other operatives to take Sukarno's body from the field.

"Wait!" Sage gently slipped the sapphire studded headband from Indra, kissing her forehead. Then, she pulled her favorite bohemian scarf from around her own neck and placed it ever so gently over Indra's face and chest.

"Safe travels to the other side, my dear friend. I'll come looking for you one day …"

With this solemn expression, she struggled to join Indra's hands together in a prayerful pose on her unmoving chest. For a few seconds longer, she grasped on. Then, an unseen light touch fell on the very top of Sage's head. It lingered just long enough … Then, she released Indra, and with it, her spirit.

A stiff breeze blew Sage's hair across her sandy, tear-stained face. Barely breathing, she teetered with the breeze, rocking back, resting on her heels. She heard nothing. The sight before her melted away.

"Sage, Sage," Cy soothed, holding her upright while jostling her upper body. "Sage, your daughter needs you. It's Gabe."

Unable to fully comprehend, she allowed Cy to help her to her feet. With ears still ringing from the blast, she was dazed and weak. He pointed about fifty yards away, and they carefully picked their way through concrete chunks and debris.

Cali was tearfully bent over Gabe. Thankfully however, Sage spied Gabe moving an arm as he evidently spoke to Cali and medics. Sage wondered, how many others we love are wounded or worse?

In the near distance, Kalen, Zia, and Carson were taking long hurried strides toward Cali and Gabe. Seeing his family well-tended, Cyprus gave Sage's arm a squeeze and left her side.

Moving closer, it was clear Gabe's shoulder and arm had been impacted by flying shrapnel. The severity of trauma was difficult to discern, but three medics were tending him with haste.

Sage knelt adjacent to Cali drawing her daughter's attention from Gabe.

"Mom, you're okay! The last seismic roll scared us all. Gabe saw I was in trouble and ran toward me. I was staggering, so disoriented by the blast and wind that I couldn't hear or see. He'd barely grabbed my waist when he was hit." She sighed heavily. "He's my hero."

Cali ever so gently squeezed Gabe's hand. The uninjured arm nearest to her now had an intravenous line.

Carson, Kalen, and Zia arrived just when Cali proclaimed Gabe to be her hero. Cut to the quick, Carson stood stoically, thinking ... I could have been the one running to save her if I hadn't been rounded up, punched out, and removed from the op by the feds. So it goes. I need to be here for her — whatever she needs. I committed to letting her choose without pressure.

With that thought, the wind turned to lighter breezes and the air began to clear. Carson felt himself relax. The people he cared for and knew were all going to recover. As far as the impact on the hacienda, he'd know for certain when he returned. No calls, no telepathic messaging was likely a positive sign.

Zane and Nate remained at the tent where several of them had been carefully dropped like a row of dolls. Unlike Zia and Carson, they were entranced by the movements of the special operatives still bustling about the field, and by whatever conversation they could glean. Almost an hour ago, they were casually conversing in the open green space of a peaceful campus. The enormity of what just occurred was both mind-boggling and numbing.

Too, Zane remained unsteady after his takedown by the agent. Sensing the attack and not knowing friend from foe, Zane had instinctively gone full force into martial art mode. Only, his adversary knew a bit more than he did. Their strength was likely equal, but Zane lacked a lightning-quick disabling maneuver. Thus, Zane's body simply ached from a swift throwdown. Now, watching how the agents worked with dexterity and certainty was every bit of Hollywood entertaining.

Evidently, there'd been a team of mercenaries sent to ensure the three thugs assigned to infiltrate and secure the product were successful. However, the FSPA discovered the sneaky invasion of the miscreants even before Sukarno's warning. The agency's brightest had anticipated such an event. The mercenaries, who believed they'd be escorting jubilant comrades with bots and storm device in-hand to a nearby aircraft, were instead incapacitated and removed from the premises.

Agent Desai continued communications with his field operatives. The medics had the open space of *TIA* and *T-Scape* triaged and managed. A small team of agents identified tunnel debris and possibly the remains of three darkly clad bodies. Portable forensics would verify soon.

Now, crews swarmed the hollow shell of the renowned biotech firm. With structural engineers and crisis experts in tow, the tedious process of looking for more injured was underway. At the same time, experts in bot technology were dragged through the building taking great pains to identify what remained and what needed to be quickly secured and removed.

Unbeknownst to most, the C-suite executives plotted with the FSPA in advance of today's heist. Knowing the international intrusion and pilfering were coming, they let it play out to catch the thieves. After all, they had Indra Sukarno on their team playing what she did best — double agent.

The FSPA just hadn't anticipated this outcome. Ending Ethos and the myriad versions and prototypes of other BioBots had not been the plan. Nor, was it assumed the energy harmonizer device would be identified and destroyed in one fell swoop.

Agent Desai and colleagues certainly did not entertain the possibility of bot-teamers clandestinely congregating in the subterranean cellar to debate the destruction of the energy harmonizer ... just when Sukarno and thugs planned *their* descent on *Turamali Innovative Arts* to retrieve coveted BioBot and energy harmonizer technologies.

The confluence of events was uncanny and yet striking.

The concrete façade crumbles. What matters remains. Coyote telepathed the fireside amigos, the tryst & schemers, and the Adept who cared.

♦

Overwhelmed by the sudden plot twist, Sage and Bayani opened their casa to family — the tryst & schemers and fireside amigos. Accommodating as many who wanted to stay the night and into the next day was easy with a couple of bedrooms and the guest house empty.

With *TIA* severely hobbled, BioBot research and production were questionable. The targeted, near demise of Ethos threw the practice of BioBot medicine and its ethics into question. The fundamental concept of biologics development to sow intelligent life appeared precarious.

Far different than the healing of the Radiance and Assault BioBots, Ethos took on the mysterious functions of the mind. Tinkering with the brain's emotions, thoughts, and consequential decision-making process was supposed to be about healing mental health afflictions, but instead the bot altered character. Weirdly, through out-of-body experiences, it connected humans to celestial space.

The incident deeply affected those who were on campus during the terrorist invasion and explosive shock wave. Since inception, *TuramaliScape* had been the epitome of intellectual and business prosperity with a distinctive pervasive peace.

Those with an embedded EthosBot felt conflicted over news of the exposé and critical destruction of the company fortress. Weren't they in the process of being healed? Perhaps some were willing to trade a change in character to escape life-altering anxiety or depression. Still, others wanted to claw the nanobot out with haste.

Distant observers, other nations fell into shock at the news, or simply believed Ethos went too far and tragedy was inevitable. Better sooner rather than later. Many fantasized about the crystal or BioBot nuggets that surely lay scattered across the Southwest just waiting for retrieval. The mere notion was intriguing.

Having been caught in an explosion of thick dusty concrete, sand and earth, Sage and the tryst & schemers were either now slumped on furniture or the tile floor of the main casa. Most had showered and changed into clothing shared with them by the Amaris Casander family.

Too inundated with thought and worry to rest, most whispered and fidgeted, moving restlessly about the living space and outdoor patio, or joining a quiet twosome or subdued conversation with several others.

Nestled close to the chiminea wood fire, Sage, Bayani, Kehlani, Jake, and Jen huddled on the patio. Wrapped in various blankets and serapes, the adults lounged on patio furniture and cushions tossed on pavers. For the past hour, discourse was intense.

"All in agreement then?" Sage queried pulling a fluffy blanket tighter around her. "We'll tell everyone when Cy gets here."

Everyone nodded. Then silence fell, with only the light voices of youth floating past open patio doors and windows.

In the living room, Kalen and Zia were propped against

a wall on a mound of pillows. Their mops of hair were still damp from showers, and with lack of attention, Kalen's beard had become scruffier. Zia was slumped between Kalen's legs, occasionally jabbering, sometimes nodding off. Choosing to be tethered tonight, Kalen and Zia were clutching one another's wrist in a sweet figure-eight caress.

Carson sat in an oversized, generously stuffed leather chair. With her legs draped across Carson's lap, Cali's weight sat against the armrest. Finally giving in to fatigue, she scooched comfortably down until her upper body rested on his chest.

Gabe would be at *T-Care* for a couple of days. In the interim, Carson was happy to hold and console his heartthrob. Consumed by the day's episode and torn between two lovers, Cali simply melted into the comfortable embrace she knew so well. The scent of wood, leather, and a hint of smokiness filled her senses, and she drifted into slumber.

Feeling acceptance and true welcome, Zane and Nate pulled a mattress from one of the guest bedrooms and tossed it onto the tile floor within feet of Zia and Kalen. With a comforter on top, they'd made a temporary home with their portable devices and pillows. Side-by-side, they probed media posts for news and social sentiment. Their shoulders and knees knocked together as they bantered and jabbered. Like others, conversation was fervent, speculating about details and what tomorrow would bring, only to be followed by outright fatigue.

"Agent Desai, the twins' uncle, mentioned Spook," Nate whispered amusingly. "Seems their team wants in on our novel firewall and network skills."

"Right, our dual capabilities of sleuthing and original approach to hide and seek in the electronic world." Zane chuckled. "We've got jobs when we graduate."

"Dude. Kemosabe, as you and Kalen say. They want us now as consultants for the agency. I don't know about you, but this is serious stuff. For me, it's a leg-up career wise, and financially, my parents would be thrilled." Nate wondered if he should pursue the agency's interest in him.

Zane countered. "Share our skill set with an organization with interests beyond on our own? Perhaps even in conflict with our beliefs? Aren't these the guys who denied Roswell and couldn't get a handle on the original eco-bot debacle? But, it was captivating watching the special operatives work the field tonight."

"Hey, I think the history of the eco-bot reads pretty well for them. Too, we could make a difference, Zaner. Meetin' up with Agent Desai is goin' on my To Do List." Nate poked Zane, as if to encourage agreement.

Zane sighed, "In. For now. My father would love it if I joined his secretive enterprise. Besides, all those lessons he paid for in the martial arts could come in handy after all."

A knock came at the front door, and Cyprus entered the living room. His man bun drooped, and his shirt and pants had clearly encountered the same haboob of concrete dust and sand as the rest had only a few hours ago. Although his face was washed clear, he had a small bandage above his right temple and a bruise on his cheek. The backs of his hands appeared scraped.

Yet, despite being beat up by the day's adversity, Cy appeared strong and serene. When he saw the tryst & schemers nestled comfortably in pairs across the living space, he smiled broadly for the first time today. Our teens, our young headstrong adults are fine, he thought. That's an accomplishment I wasn't sure I'd pull off when they each decided to be a special operative on *my* operation.

At the esteemed agent's arrival, Carson nodded at him,

and Kalen nearly shouted, "Uncle Cy! You're here." Since Kalen didn't want to move an inch from the comfort of Zia, he simply used his free hand to hoist a loose fist in the air indicating success. Zane and Nate followed Kalen's lead with the same signal for success.

Roused from the greeting, Cali simply gazed at her uncle with a weak smile, placing her hand flat against her heart. Cyprus took in the endearing reactions and gave a special wink for Cali.

A breeze blew in from the patio bringing the scent of burning wood. In seconds, footfalls and quiet wishes of welcome followed, as the rest of the fireside amigos moved inside greeting the last of their fold.

Jen greeted her partner with a passionate never-ending hug. When she pulled back to study his eyes, she recognized the depth of exhaustion and wear. She tenderly touched his forehead and cheek.

"You're amazing Agent Desai. Being amazing in every minute, every day, takes a toll." She arched her eyebrows and shook her head. *You know exactly what I'm thinking. It's time.*

With his closest companions nearby and Jen's embrace surrounding him, Cyprus let his shoulders fall. He pulled out a bar height equipale chair and promptly sank into it.

Kehlani stood behind Cy and placed her hands on his shoulders while she closed her eyes. The warmth of Kehlani's touch filtered down through every aching muscle and up into his head relieving tension. His head fell lightly forward onto Jen's chest. In the moment, the healing presence of two Adepts was everything the federal agent needed.

Across the kitchen counter, Jake softly pushed a frothy beverage toward Cy. He'd need sustenance when he recovered from Kehlani's induced reverie.

Observing the exchange, Bayani leaned his back against a skip-peeled pole and pulled Sage by the waist toward him in a rocking embrace meant to soothe.

Coyote yipped and howled. *The four-leggeds roam in peace tonight. Second chance. We will heal. You will heal.*

Nearly startling those in the hacienda, the entire pack yipped in acknowledgement. Mysteriously, the wind whipped the patio doors to a fully open position, and with it, the warmth of the chiminea fire and glow of moonlight filtered into the room.

Kehlani let out a discernable breath. They were all free from Ethos and the weird energy harmonizer machine. For now.

Indra Sukarno is lost to us here, but she soars above our canyons. She trots with Coyote and meanders with Cougar. Sukarno has not left us. Kehlani telepathed to all in the hacienda — those wide awake, drifting, or asleep. All *heard*.

With *Coyote's* interlude and Kehlani's telepathic message, the night reset. Couples jostled awake to hear final messages.

Sage told the ensemble she was leaving *Turamali Innovative Arts*. Perhaps, she could be enticed by consultancy, but she was done with BioBots. It was time for full attention on the hacienda and the equine spirits who plodded the red rock soil.

Cy and Jen were taking an extended hiatus from agent and lawyerly roles. Long hikes across canyons and river rafting called them. Perhaps, as the adventure unfolded, Kehlani and Jake, and Sage and Bayani would join them. After all, the fireside amigos were 'all for one' and 'one for all'.

Kalen professed his love for Zia. Carson and Cali committed to always loving one another, but for now, freedom to be with others. Gabe, Carson, and Cali — all would have second chances. Zane and Nate could only follow up with a one-liner, "We're in with all of you for the long haul."

Turamali Innovative Arts socially committed to a responsible second chance in healing. Perhaps, not so much dabbling in personal ethos, but definitely healing the soma. The psyche would be left to the Adepts.

An enchanting wind blew across *TuramaliScape*. Glistening crystal shards from upended BioBots were strewn far and wide. Crystal energy with a second chance.

Not the end, but the beginning of so much more.

Books by S Sky, MS

Sage and the Crystal Bot – Desert Surge

Sage and the Crystal Bot – Telepathy Tide

Shelf Unbound 2023 Best Indie Book,
100 Top Notables Award

Sage and the Crystal Bot – Turamali Life

Desert Author, S Sky, MS

Give me warm desert breezes with the damp scent of creosote and chiminea-burning pinyon pine, and I'm in heaven. Spanish missions and sacred locales hold a special allure and mystery, and it is here I find my strength.

From our beloved four-legged companions, I gather love and soul insight. Between my daughter and I, we have several dogs. They are all sizes, all rescues, the best hiking companions, and of course, our daily cuddles. A kind-hearted paint mare who loves the English jumps and knows a few Western tricks rounds out the family.

Residing in the Southwest, I author fiction and nonfiction. Sage and the Crystal Bot trilogy was soul-driven, as I engage readers to ponder our fragile Earth and the choices we make. EthosBot builds on concepts in the trilogy, extending the escapade to youth and further probing the moral implications of the choices we make.

Much of what I compose is based on real science and the rest is artistry. I hope you are inspired to explore what's real in this novel and what is slightly twisted. Most of all, enjoy the characters and the nonstop adventure. To those who read my work, I am honored.

Amazon.com/author/desert-author-ss

Made in the USA
Middletown, DE
01 April 2024

52209109R00139